HAWKS EFFECT · VOLUME 1 · EPISODE 1

Rael Wissdorf · Nicholas Hede · Frank J. Williams III

Hawks Effect

Volume 1 · Episode 1

One Last Con

Trivocum Verlag

TRIVOCUM PRESS
Copyright © 2017 by Rael Wissdorf, Nicholas Hede, Frank J. Williams III
ISBN: 978-3-946797-08-1
All Rights Reserved
Second Print Edition: October 2017

Edited by Chris Naumann & Nehemiah Inverse
Cover Art by Sarah Richter
www.sarah-richter-illustration.de
The author's website:
hawks-seffect.com

Dedicated to Harry Evers.
May angels guide you to your rest.

Prologue

Something wasn't right. Of course, Galicia couldn't tell what exactly, just a feeling that she had missed something. She had been working for six hours now, and the loud whirring of the seemingly ancient computer system that filled the entire room made it difficult to concentrate. The machinery had been in place since the 1950's and the keyboard and monitor that she was using had given her a headache hours ago. The antiquated keyboard in particular, with its full weighted keys with little room between them, was most problematic. Each keystroke took effort and she hadn't stopped typing since she sat down. After two hours she developed blisters. Now they were slick with spots of blood mixed with serum. The oppressive heat of the desert air, even in the middle of the night, combined with the heat generated from the dusty computer system to create a furnace in the office. So she couldn't be sure if she had indeed missed something or if her mind was playing tricks on her. Still, the feeling persisted. But she had come too far now to stop, and she knew she was running out of time.

Galicia wiped sweat from her brow to keep it from dripping into her eyes. At her side, she heard a familiar shuffling and an audible sigh come from her partner. "You're doing it again," she said plainly.

"Sorry, sorry," came the response from Sinza Flanagan. She walked over to Galicia's shoulder and looked intently at the computer screen. It was filled with a blur of text that she couldn't hope to understand. "It's just that it's been six hours. I didn't expect it to take this long. And the heat here! God!"

Galicia looked up at Sinza and rolled her eyes, never missing a keystroke. "We are in the desert, love. What did you expect?"

"Not six hours! She never told us it would take this long. And she also didn't tell us the goddamn computer was from the Space Race." Sinza looked at Galicia, who was wiping sweat from her brow once again. "I'm sorry Gal. I've been standing here complaining this whole time and you're the one doing all the work." She placed her hands on Galicia's shoulders and gave them a quick rub. Galicia rolled her neck and closed her eyes. The bloody keys brought a frown to Sinza's face. "Can't you take a break for just a little bit?"

"I'm almost there Sinz. You know we don't have the time. Someone could have detected us hours ago and sent teams after us. She said they were monitoring this place." Galicia paused her typing for a brief second and reached up to squeeze Sinza's hand. They both gave a halfhearted smile before Galicia continued her work. Sinza moved over to a barred window and stared out into the desert night. The silhouette of the mesas broke through the starlight in the distance, and the town below, if it could be called a town, was silent as a tomb. An old, abandoned Sinclair gas station with its iconic green dinosaur sat across from their warehouse, and for a brief second, Sinza thought she saw a light coming from inside. She instinctively reached for her sidearm, but as her eyes refocused, the light was gone. Had she imagined it? Both women had been at this for six hours now, and they were exhausted. Perhaps she was losing her edge.

Galicia glanced over when she saw Sinza tense and reach for the weapon. In her skin-tight black incursion suit, Galicia thought that Sinza looked like a panther, ready to strike. Her body was toned and athletic, even muscular by female standards, and the snug suit formed to the curves of her body like a second skin. Her years in the Army had formed her body into a perfect machine for many types of work, but usually not the silent type. It took a lot of convincing to get Sinza to sneak into the warehouse instead of kicking down the door, pistols drawn. So far there had been no resistance, but Galicia feared for anyone who crossed paths with her partner. The suit matched her shortly cropped black hair, which, in a certain light, had a sheen to it that appeared like raven's feathers; a deep black that Galicia was envious of. Her own golden hair was usually cut short, just below the chin, but in the past few months, she had let it grow out. In this heat, she was now regretting that decision. Her hair was a tangled sweaty mop that she tried not to think about.

"See anything?" Galicia asked.

"I thought I did, but I don't know. This place is weird."

"I know what you mean."

"I didn't expect it to look so, familiar," Sinza said. "I mean, there is a Sinclair gas station over there. How is that possible?"

"She told us this had been created purposefully. But I didn't expect this."

Sinza walked the office again. It was a glass-enclosed structure that overlooked the warehouse floor. Wooden crates were stacked haphazardly and a row of enclosed offices lined the south wall. This manager's office oversaw everything, and from this vantage, Sinza could see each part of the warehouse.

"Sinz, I've almost got it," Galicia said with a sigh. Sinza rushed to the desk and stared hopefully at the confusing monitor.

"How can you tell?"

"I just can."

A sharp crackling noise brought their attention to the north window. Sinza ran to it and Galicia peered over her monitor. "Get out of the way," Galicia shouted to Sinza over the din of the crackling. Sinza scooted to the side. Hovering about three meters off the floor, a white ball of energy had emerged from thin air. The crackling emanated from bolts of electricity shooting out from its center and striking another pile of wooden crates on the warehouse floor. Dust from the floor swirled as it was lifted from the ground below the energy ball until it was finally drawn inside the phenomenon.

"Is that supposed to happen?" Sinza asked, never looking away.

"I hope so," Galicia said. Her fingers had never left the keyboard. She focused now on the monitor and with a heavy sigh, she pressed the final key. "Done."

The white ball of energy below grew to five feet in diameter in the blink of an eye before transforming into a column of blinding white energy that erupted into the night sky. The glass windows shattered and crates below were blown to splinters. The column flowed with power melting a hole in the roof of the warehouse in the process. There was no telling how high up it went. Sinza had rushed to shield Galicia behind the desk and both women peeked over the top. The column roared with power and the noise was deafening. It grew even louder, as the winds picked up speed, and both women crouched low while covering their ears. And in an instant, it was gone. Falling glass, wood, and metal were left in its wake. The computer monitor went blank, save for a blinking green cursor. The partners stood from behind the desk and surveyed the damage.

"What the hell was that?" Sinza asked. "She never said it would do that."

Galicia peered through the office windows, now simply holes in the walls. The shop floor had been scorched black to match the radius of the energy column. She looked up. The roof had a perfect circle melted out, with the edges still glowing orange. But the column itself hadn't radiated heat. She moved back to the desk and began typing.

"Was that it? Did we do it?" Sinza asked. Neither seemed entirely sure of what to expect, but Sinza had begun to hope.

"No," Galicia said. "No no no no." Her face was painted with worry as she typed. "It's still active," she said, lifting her face to Sinza.

"What? How can that be? What was that thing we just saw?"

"I don't know."

"But that had to do it! That had to shut it down," Sinza said, pointing to the wreckage.

"I don't know," came the response again. "I don't know, okay!" she shouted. Her shoulders sagged and she began to sob. The hours of work had drained Galicia and this ambiguous conclusion left her emotionally distraught.

"Hey, Gal, listen," Sinza said, rushing to her partner. She placed her hands on her shoulders. "You did good, you know that right?" Galicia shrugged. "It's got to be this machinery. The sensors must have fried. There is no way it's still open." Galicia looked up at Sinza. Tears streaked the sweat on her face. Sinza wiped them away. "None of that now. We just go back to see her. She'll confirm it for us, you'll see."

"Okay Sinz," Galicia replied weakly. She sniffed and wiped the last tear away and stood tall. "Okay," she repeated smiling. Sinza always brought out the best in her.

A beeping at the commando's belt instantly soured the mood.   Sinza's smile disappeared, as she deftly removed the monitor from her waist, and scanned the display.

"We've got movement outside. Closing fast."

Galicia turned back to the computer and began typing. "How long do I have?"

"Less than a minute," Sinza replied, issuing an apologetic look.

"A minute! Bloody hell, I need twenty to extract the program."

"You've got a minute. Think of something fast. I'll give you as much time as I can."

"Who is it?" Galicia asked.

"I can't tell. Approaching from all sides, but their focus is on the north wall," she said, gesturing towards the rubble and scorched circular floor. "They're smart though - SpecOps whoever it is."

"It's not enough time," Galicia said. She closed her eyes for a brief second. "I can't extract the program, and you can't carry all this machinery. I'll wipe our tracks. We'll have to start all over though."

"No, we won't! It worked Gal, I believe in you. Just cover us so they can't trace the program back to her," Sinza said. Pistols in hand, she was ready for battle.

"It'll take time."

"I said I'd give you as much as I can, but when we go, we go," Sinza barked in a strict authoritative tone. Galicia nodded. Sinza trusted her, and she trusted Sinza. This was what she was best at. She got to work on the computer as Sinza leaped through the broken window to the shop floor below, taking cover behind a shattered crate. A second glance at the sensor showed the forces huddled around the wall beyond. The attack would come any second now. "Get ready!" she shouted to Galicia.

An explosion rocked the building as the soldiers breached the wall. Galicia instinctively ducked but rose again just enough to work on the computer while not exposing herself to gunfire. Smoke and debris filled the air below and a metallic hockey puck skidded across the floor to Sinza's feet. "Goddamnit!" she said, staring at the device. She quickly dropped her guns and unbuckled her belt just before the device emitted a blue light and her weapons and ammunition were drawn instantly to the device's magnetic gravity well. She could tell from the footfalls that the soldiers had moved to surround her, but none had made it to the southern side of the building yet. Expertly, she rolled back to find new cover and moved to one side. Better to take them on one at a time than to have to fight the group in the center.

She moved quickly and quietly to the first soldier, grabbing his gun and lifting it as she issued a knife hand thrust to his throat before smashing his face against a nearby crate. He collapsed to the floor hard, landing face first against the concrete. Upon impact, a bloody tooth flew from his open mouth, skittering along the flat surface before coming to rest several meters away.

The noise brought the attention of the other soldiers, but she was already on the move. Gunfire exploded into the crates, and Sinza noticed the small barbed projectiles peppering the wood were not bullets but incapacitating bolts. With precision, she slid from soldier to soldier, disarming and rendering them unconscious one after the other.

Galicia heard the commotion below and worked as fast as she could. Her vision was now illuminated red, and she paused at the ancient keyboard to view a virtual keyboard floating in the space in front of her. She quickly made gestures at certain odd symbols located on the hexagonal virtual keys before shaking her head to clear the image and getting back to the real keys in front of her. Her fingers now moved with an inhuman speed while the machinery on the wall behind her began to spark and smoke. She was focused, and the gunfire below did not stun her or break her concentration. Even with her bolstered speed, she still needed time to finish.

The guards against the western wall were dispatched, and half a dozen stood on the east, all weapons trained on her crate. Sinza couldn't move out without being riddled by the small electric barbs. That left her with only one option. "Gal!" she shouted at the top of her lungs. "Iron Hide!" Galicia paused her keystrokes with her right hand, continuing with her left. The red keyboard floated in front of her once again, and with her right hand, she tapped the necessary symbols. The walls turned to a wireframe view and she saw a skeletal image of Sinza trapped behind the crate with the guards closing in. A few more taps and Galicia had a ball of golden yellow energy in her palm. She threw it through the walls to Sinza. With her task completed, the wireframe image receded, the red keyboard disappeared, and both her hands went back to the ancient input device.

Sinza felt the energy strike her frame and looked at her arms. A golden sheen coated every inch of her body, causing her to smile. "Now we can have some fun," she said, grinning devilishly. She emerged confidently from behind the safety of the crate into a hail of gunfire. The barbs struck her form and fell harmlessly to the floor, with each impact creating tiny golden ripples along the shield. Emboldened, Sinza charged the soldiers and engaged them all at once. A swift knee to the helmet shattered the visor of one and sent him flailing back into a crate. She blocked a palm strike from another and ducked under his follow up punch, twisting arms and countering with her own spinning heels. Two more down. Knives appeared in the hands of the three remaining soldiers. One rushed her while the others kept two paces back. She sprung backward, avoiding his slashes while blocking a sudden thrust to her abdomen with a sweep of her arm. Clasping the soldier's forearm, she twisted the wrist until the knife fell to the ground, and kicked the soldier in the ribs so hard that he flew backward, landing in a heap against a box of rusted machinery. Sinza picked up the knife and prepared to address her remaining opponents, a man, and a woman. The duo rushed her simultaneously from the right and left. Rolling out of the way, she slashed at her closest opponent. He deftly blocked her strike while the second soldier slashed her exposed right side. The golden body shield flashed brightly upon contact, easily turning away the blade, while the force of the attack reverberated just above her torso. It had saved her, but wouldn't last more than one more direct strike. Grabbing the arm of her first assailant, she flipped him over her head, landing him between her and the female soldier. A swift strike with the pommel of her knife against his temple stunned him, giving her a moment to twist his body around and bring her knee up to his chin, knocking him unconscious. She shoved the crumpling form aside as the final soldier attacked.

This one was fast! An expert at knife combat herself, Sinza was hard pressed to match this woman's speed. Both fighters were ablur with motion, as metal flashed and raised sparks as the two blades made repeated contact. Seizing the tiniest of openings, the soldier sliced at Sinza's torso, and her golden shield flickered weakly before winking out of existence. As her assailant moved in for the kill, Sinza slipped aside and slashed her forearm, causing the weapon to fall. Seeing her chance, she lunged forward and stabbed toward the woman's throat. An inch from her target, Sinza's knife was suddenly flung from her hand with the force of a bullet and buried itself deep into the metal wall behind her.   Undaunted, she fired a quick elbow instead, catching the woman with a hard blow to the jaw, instantly dropping her to the floor.

The knife flying from her hand was no accident. They had an Initiator. A long slow scraping noise came from the breach in the wall. This was no knife being drawn from a sheath, but a sword. Through the dust and smoke, she recognized the image of stark white hair and a red illuminated face to its side.

"Gal! Move now!" Sinza knew who these two were and she knew she stood no chance, especially not here. Galicia had finished her Hack, obtaining what info she could while covering her tracks. With a final keystroke, the office went dark, followed by several pops and flashes as the ancient computer's hard drive and CPU melted into slag. The shout from Sinza was perfectly timed as the blonde hacker stepped onto the catwalk and leaped over the railing landing easily on the warehouse floor.   She heard Sinza's feet running towards her, and together the two sprinted toward the hallway.

"Who is it?" Galicia asked as they ran.

"It's Aeternus. Gavrael, and Hanzoh. I know the sound of that sword being drawn anywhere."

"Bloody hell," Galicia swore. "Well, we can't fight them, but I can slow them down."

"Good idea. We'll use this smaller corridor. Once you're done we'll head to the end of the main hallway, and slip through the exit door."

Galicia nodded and they approached the short office hall. Galicia's vision glowed red and as they passed the first door, she tapped her red keys and the walls of the passage illuminated for ten meters before fading after they passed. She did this twice more before the duo emerged into the center of the main office corridor. The passage to the left ended abruptly at a large file cabinet resting against the wall, while the opening to the right led past a collection of office doors toward Sinza's predetermined exit. Quickly, the pair sprinted to the far door and turned the knob, only to find it locked. A faint red glow emanated from around the doorframe, causing Galicia to swear in frustration.

"Dammit! Not only is it locked, but it's shielded with a Fortress code."

"Can you Hack it?" Sinza asked.

"Sure, if I had 30 freakin' minutes," Galicia replied in aggravation, kicking the shielded door for good measure. "Or enough CCE for a Blast."

A low tone from her Visor informed that their pursuers had sprung the first trap. The first ten meters of the walls in the smaller corridor exploded with countless spikes and projections from either side, aimed at skewering her pursuers. While the trap was quick and dirty, her visor informed her none of the spikes had hit their intended target. These two men were better than that of course, but it was worth a try. The only positive was that it did slow them down for the moment.

"Bollocks!"

"C'mon!" Sinza exclaimed, grabbing the arm of her partner. "Try the offices on the right. They're on the outer edge of the building. If we're lucky, We can get out through a window!"

The two tried several doors as they made their way back the way they came, but the results were just as fruitless. Each door opened into a windowless room used for storing office supplies or equipment. Without explosives, the women were blocked from escaping the building. Even more problematic was the fact that each door they tried took them closer and closer to their pursuers.

The final door had a sign above it that read "Women." Elation turned into frustration once again when they discovered the door to the bathroom was locked. At the same time, another tone informed them that Galicia's second trap had been sprung.

"Shit!" Sinza yelled.

Both women pressed their shoulders against the door, but it wouldn't budge. A subtle inspection by Galicia visor revealed that this door was coded as well, but in a way that she had never seen before. It was an old augmentation had been erected a long time ago. So long in fact that it appeared to be degrading, revealing flaws in its code.

"I can Hack this!" Galicia exclaimed. "I just need a little time."

The two pursuing soldiers had cleared the spike trap and moved forward with caution. Suddenly the one with the visor yelled, "Jump three meters forward!" The instant they sprang, the floor disappeared beneath their feet, opening up into a black chasm of unknown depth, but the smaller soldier' senses were sharp. He read the trap even before receiving confirmation from his visor, and the two men cleared it with ease.

"Got them!" the blonde exclaimed.

Just beyond the abyss, Galicia's third and final snare activated. Knowing that the two capable soldiers would sense the floor trap, she set the final one with that intent in mind. The two men had blundered into a stasis field, unable to move, unable to blink.

"That'll hold them for a bit, but my visor is running low on power, and I have to crack this door while keeping those two at bay at the same time."

"I'll do what I can to give you some time, but you gotta get that lock sprung Gal," Sinza whispered to her companion.

"Just monitor them. If their Initiator makes any moves to Hack my field, let me know."

Sinza walked the short distance toward the intersecting hall, while Galicia tapped several keys on her virtual keyboard sending Core Conversion Energy streaming into the bathroom door. She tapped again, this time using a larger amount of her energy, and the field around the door slowly began to weaken.

Drawing her pistol, the raven-haired commando rounded the corner and abruptly stopped. An invisible wall one foot thick stood between her and the two men, who hung, suspended mid-air in Galicia's trap. She knew it wouldn't last for long, but hopefully, it would give Sinza the time she needed. Perhaps a distraction would slow their attempts at escape as well.

"You know, I heard stories about you two," Sinza began. "Gavrael and Hanzoh, the sword and the shield. What I don't understand is why you continue to hunt us like dogs."

The trapped soldiers glared at the woman but kept silent.

"You are being manipulated, and you don't even know it. But I gotta believe you are more than just mindless grunts, following orders instead of thinking for yourselves."

Eyes narrowed as the men took in her words. Still, they remained silent.

"Nothing to say? I was told you are both reasonable men; noble even. Do you even know why you're here?"

"I am here to stop two terrorists from destroying my world," the white-haired Gavrael said. His voice was low and serious, accusing while being even. "I would say there is no greater good, nothing nobler than that."

"We are not terrorists!" Sinza shouted vehemently.

"The righteous blood of monks and innocents spilled by your handiwork says otherwise," the white-haired soldier retorted. "The spirits of those whose lives you cut short cry out against you."

"Those two incidents in Kohai; the Transit Tower disaster, and the destruction of Asakusa Temple were tragic and horrible, but our presence at the time was purely coincidental. Yes, we were there, but not to damage property or hurt anyone. We were…gathering intelligence at the time, nothing more."

Gavrael slowly shook his head.

"I have seen the vids; I have examined the crime scenes. I have talked to one of my own soldiers whom you both attacked. His report tells me all I need to know about your actions and the explosions left in your wake."

His tone was flat with a touch of sadness. Sinza noted that while he was direct, there was no anger shown during this exchange. His emotions did not rule him here. This made him deadly. A focused opponent was a dangerous one.

"Well, the soldiers yeah," Sinza said, conciliatorily. "We engaged, but we didn't kill him. We didn't kill anyone. Ask your man. Take a look at your vids with a critical eye. Is there even one instance of us killing a single person? We attacked and incapacitated your soldiers, that's true. But no deaths, ever."

"Thousands of people injured, hundreds of lives lost, and you tell me you had nothing to do with any of it? Unbelievable. The evidence—"

"...Was fabricated!" Sinza shouted. "Someone set us up, probably because we made such an easy target. Can't you see? This goes against everything we are trying to do. We're trying to save people, not hurt them!"

"I've seen the bodies personally," Gavrael responded. "Every one of those broken, burned, mutilated corpses."

"Those deaths are not on my shoulders, or Galicia's. Our intentions are peaceful."

"I suppose that shaft of light that tore through this structure minutes ago happened all by itself. Major Flanagan please, your lies are as transparent as glass."

"We are telling the truth!" Sinza exclaimed. You're being used, Gavrael, you and your entire Cluster. Someone is lying to you."

"On that, we agree. The question is, do I trust the words of my oldest friends and mentors, including the Grandmaster of my Cluster, or do I trust the word of a woman who has been wreaking havoc across Nedara? The answer is obvious. Hanzoh?"

"I'm in, boss!"

"What's happening?" Galicia cried out suddenly. "I'm losing control over the field!"

Sinza had been so focused on Gavrael, that she hadn't noticed Hanzoh's subtle movements. By pressing his temple against his left shoulder, the Initiator depressed a stud in his visor, switching the display into "free-form" mode. Using his eyes, the sergeant had positioned the virtual keyboard just below his left hand. While Sinza and Gavrael were speaking, he slowly tapped out a sequence of characters.

"Galicia hurry, they're breaking free!" Sinza shouted. She watched in horror as the two men slowly moved through the stasis field as if trapped in tar. Little by little, Gavrael began to unsheathe his sword, and with each passing moment, their movements became faster and easier. Turning her back on Gavrael and Hanzoh, she rushed back to the bathroom door to see a weakened Galicia bathed in sweat as she continued to Hack into the door's code.

"We've got about a minute, Gal. How much power is left?"

"I'm at two percent, but I think I've got it."

Sinza saw that a soft blue light had appeared around the edges of the door. Moments later it began pulsating wildly, while the door itself began to vibrate.

Hearing a sound, she turned her head and gasped.

Booted feet landed gently on the floor as the stasis field began to die around their two pursuers.

"Seconds Gal!"

"Almost there..."

The sword in Gavrael's hand began to attract energy from the field, as the runes lining the ink black blade began to glow brightly. He was drawing off the stasis. Moments later, the field dissipated, and the two men rounded the corner at full speed.

"Galicia!" Sinza screamed.

The bathroom door flew open and the women dove inside, quickly slamming it shut behind them. The lock engaged just as the two men forced their shoulders into the door. It soundly repelled their advance, throwing them both off balance. As the soldiers prepared for another assault, they heard a shout coming from inside the room, as an intense blue light erupted from under the door. After two more attempts, they burst inside and were astonished to find the bathroom empty.

Their quarry had vanished!

Chapter 1

The fateful moment between life and death is often measured by fractions of an inch. This time it arrived in the shape of an ambulance hurtling towards the young woman who had just stepped onto a crosswalk of a busy intersection in London's East End. Distracted by her deep thoughts, she didn't hear the blaring rise and fall of the vehicle's siren as she started to walk across the street. The ambulance driver, catching sight of her at the very last second, jerked the steering wheel and hit the brakes with a screech of tires. At the sound the woman's head snapped up and, recognizing the danger, she jumped back toward the sidewalk as the rescue vehicle narrowly missed hitting her. As it came to a skidding halt a large gout of water rose in its wake, thoroughly soaking the startled woman. Visibly shaken, she turned and looked inside the window of the vehicle and saw the angry ambulance driver shaking a fist at her through the opening.

"Watch your arse you bloody tart! You tryin' to get us both killed?" the burly man shouted. Finally, the ambulance sped off with its siren wailing away, splitting the mass of vehicles ahead of it like Moses parting the Red Sea.

"Bloody close," Laurina whispered, shaking the dirty water from her oversized leather coat. Her reddish brown hair was uncovered and soaked by the continuous drizzle thanks to her own forgetfulness. The red flat cap that she usually wore lay atop the bureau in the bedroom of her Virgil Street flat, in London Town. She already felt like a mess, and now this. Blood throbbed in her temples as she railed at her own inattentiveness.

Twit! Mind your eyes; otherwise, you'll never get this mystery solved!

After a few calming breaths, she quickly recovered from her shock and continued on her way. She pushed through the hectic throng of people crowding the sidewalk until she reached a corner. Ducking into one of London's quieter side streets, she walked several blocks until she arrived at the entrance of an old brownstone a few minutes later. Bounding up the wet stairs, Laurina stood in front of the familiar tall oak great door, with the large antique knocker that resembled the face of a gargoyle. As she reached for the handle, a familiar voice greeted her ears.

"You know, you really should undress first before taking a bath," a jovial voice quipped as the door swung open. "It's a lot more effective."

A beefy young man wearing faded jeans and a rumpled brown cardigan sweater stood inside the apartment grinning from ear to ear.

"Very funny, Abel", Laurina replied shaking her head ruefully. "After seeing a half-drowned woman seeking sanctuary at your doorstep, one might think that a gallant man would respond with compassion instead of jokes at her expense. And if that woman happened to be your own sister, one would think that a man of honor would be even more welcoming! But no, I have to be stuck with a brutish clod for a brother."

"Ah m'lady, you've cut me to the quick," Abel said, throwing a hand over his heart as he stepped away from the door.

Waving her inside, he added with a bit of chagrin, "Forgive me, Laur. I know I can be an oaf at times. Do come in please."

"How's your pain today?" she asked, shaking the water from her shoulders as she stepped into the foyer.

"I've been better. The doctor's been talking about stepping me up to Oxycontin, but I won't hear of it. I'd rather be in pain with most of my faculties intact than take that poison and lose my mind. It's bad enough I have to take these."

He pulled a white medicine bottle from his pants pocket and showed it to Laurina. Blinking rainwater from her eyes, she scanned it, seeing the word Vicotin in bold letters.

"Poor Abel," she sighed.

"This bloody rain isn't helping matters either, I'll tell you that."

"Well, it's not doing me any favors either, as you can see."

"Quite," the big man replied, as he grabbed his wolf's head cane and limped toward the kitchenette. "I'll put the kettle on."

Several minutes later after shucking and hanging up her wet coat in the foyer, and after accepting a towel from her older brother, Laurina was hard at work sitting in his tiny kitchen, drying off and reclaiming her appearance. After toweling her soaked hair dry, she had just begun to comb it back into style when Abel limped over to the table with a tray of tea he had prepared. Leaning heavily on his cane, the big man settled his bulk into the seat across from her. After pouring a cup for each of them, he waited patiently, blowing over his steaming beverage while she added the finishing touches to her hair. Once that chore was finished, they sat face to face in the kitchenette in silence. Abel had seated himself in front of an incredibly grimy window which allowed only an extremely foggy view of the docks in the background. Laurina smiled as she remembered how she always used to pull his leg about how dirty his windows were, which merely prompted him to reply in a surly voice, "It's useless to obsess about it. Dirt is the only constant in this part of the world"

Peering through that window, Laurina could barely make out the form of a container ship being loaded, and in the foreground, the rotting courtyard of a shipping company where ancient white paint flaked off its wooden framework. A signal horn bellowed mournfully into the damp air like the call of a great seafaring god; reminding the dockworkers in a language that she didn't understand that the docks were always full of secrets.

The view notwithstanding, Laurina found that she liked Abel's flat; his tiny, shabby kitchen, and the funky worn linoleum on the floor. It featured several holes the size of the palm of her hand, which allowed you to see clear through to the screed below. She found that she was also fond of the cheap kitchen furniture; the mismatched red vinyl covered chair that she sat upon, the worn-out wooden corner seat that he preferred, and the Formica-topped dining table laden with newspapers. Then there was his exquisite bone-china service and the quaint little tea-warmer with its tiny flickering flame. Such finery which would normally seem out of place in this neighborhood, somehow fit well within her older brother's eclectic scheme, just like everything else he owned.

Abel Hawks worked as a researcher and consultant at Hatchard's Booksellers, the oldest and most prestigious bookstore in London. Even at 30 years old he was considered an expert in rare tomes, and as such, a number of first editions were in evidence in nearly every corner of his flat. He even had bookshelves in the kitchen reserved for the less valuable acquisitions, placed high on the wall below the ceiling. The remainder of the flat, three small rooms, was packed with novels (mostly paperbacks) that he read strictly for pleasure, acquired at a substantial discount. A voracious reader, Abel never met a book he didn't like, and since he had ready access to them at the shop, he rarely left work without one. When he wasn't reading, the remainder of his free time was spent in front of the computer.

I couldn't ask for a more loving and supportive brother, but Gawd, you are such a nerd!

Laurina smiled as she wistfully admired his coal black hair, which he wore clipped extremely short. In the front, it ran along his forehead forming a "V" in the center; a style most referred to as a Widow's Peak. Had his face been thinner, it would have given him a more sinister appearance, making him more attractive to women who loved the 'bad boy" type. Not that he was unattractive to the average woman, but his round face made him look more like a British version of Charlie Brown. While most people would call Abel fat at 300 pounds, in truth he was just big all over; a product of both healthy genes and his sedentary lifestyle. And while he had proven resistant to any type of weight-loss diet, he always seemed to be comfortable with himself and his appearance. Except for his disability, that is.

While on his first business trip in Ireland ten years earlier, Abel had his left leg shattered after being struck by a lorry, as he attempted to rescue a little girl who had fallen in the road. Even though the child had escaped serious injury, he had not been as fortunate. During his hospital stay, he experienced a setback to his condition after contracting a staph infection that nearly killed him. He endured a dozen different surgeries and many months in rehab, but thanks to the support of his sisters, he had finally recovered.   Unfortunately due to extensive nerve damage, the large number of pins and bolts used in his leg, and the onset of arthritis, pain had become an ever-present and unwelcome companion in his life. Though he never regretted saving the life of that child, thoughts of how the accident had changed his life for the worse, occasionally made him bitter about his fate.

He appeared to be an intimidating figure, large of body and bone, with heavy black brows that were almost joined, making him capable of casting a fearsome scowl when angered. In reality, he was tender-hearted and mild-mannered; still retaining the mischievous twinkle in his dark green eyes from childhood. Laurina wondered whether it was his lack of an aggressive nature or his disability that was the reason for his lack of success with the opposite sex. Knowing the measure of the man like she did, any woman's rejection of her brother certainly didn't speak well of their character.

Clearing his throat, more to get her attention than anything else, Abel made an exaggerated show of looking up and down at her figure.

"I see that you're dressed in that alarmingly sexy way again," he said, frowning while wagging his finger back and forth. "Don't tell me that you're once again off to bullshit another poor chap?"

Laurina looked down at herself and smiled in spite of where she knew this conversation was headed. She had to agree that the black fish-net stockings under her black leather miniskirt were designed specifically to make a man's head spin. Her shapely legs enhanced the effect even more.

"Abel, I'm wearing my working clothes as you can see," she said smiling tentatively. "And yes, I do have plans for later, if you must know."

"You know how that bothers me," he replied with irritation. "You had so much promise."

Laurina sighed heavily, shaking her head.

Here we go again.

It was true from the beginning that Laurina Hawks had shown much promise as a ballet dancer. Dame Adelaide Thome, the 75-year-old former Principle dancer of the Royal Ballet, and current director of the Dorchester School of Dance once told her that she had to potential to be the "next big thing" if she worked hard at the craft.

"You have skill and talent, my dear," she had said. "That much is evident. But talent is not enough. Motivation and the will to be the best are what's necessary for a dancer to truly succeed. Dig deep and cultivate these qualities within yourself, and will realize your dreams."

Following that advice, Laurina found her dedication and practiced faithfully. In time, she passed her Solo Seal examination through the Royal Academy of Dance with distinction. Soon after finishing her exam, she was thrilled to receive an offer for the lead in a local production of Cinderella, in which she performed admirably. The following year was even better when she was awarded the role of principal dancer in the Dorchester Dance Troupe's production of Swan Lake.

She had even received a favorable write up in the local paper, which thrilled Abel and Galicia to no end.

Laurina thought sure that her star would continue to rise, and that success as a part of a major ballet company would be just around the corner. Unfortunately, that success never came.

A sharp decline in Britain's economy led to problems with providing funding for the Arts. As a result, a large number of mid-sized ballet companies, including the Dorchester Dance Troupe became casualties of the economic downturn and closed their doors. This led to a large influx of talented dancers vying for the small number of major appointments that remained. The competition was fierce and each audition Laurina attended seemed only to end in disappointment when she received news that another dancer had claimed the coveted spot.

Several times Laurina auditioned herself into becoming one of two remaining candidates for a major appointment; once with the Birmingham Royal Ballet and the other with the English National Ballet. Each time, she left the audition hall in bitter disappointment after her rival was chosen instead of her. Missing the final cut after auditioning for the London Ballet was particularly heartbreaking. Each experience made her question whether she had the heart to remain in the profession. One day Laurina awoke to find that she had become disillusioned after so many failures. It was the lowest point in her life.

"Abel, I know you want me to continue to try to make one of the major ballet companies, but working in the small dance troupes while waiting for another chance to audition, doesn't pay the bills," she sighed.

Neither did working as an exotic dancer.

Back when her brother suffered his accident, times were tough on the Hawks family. Through a legal technicality, the lorry driver and his company were not held liable for his injuries, citing that Abel, "knowingly and willingly" ran in front of the vehicle. The five thousand pounds that they finally offered was termed a "goodwill gesture" that his lawyer advised him to accept. The thirty-five hundred pounds that remained after the barrister's fee, was immediately eaten up by Abel's mounting medical bills. His short-term disability was running out, and he hadn't been at his new job long enough to qualify for long-term disability. Meanwhile, their younger sister Galicia needed money to continue her nursing classes, and she was having difficulty managing the demands of her entry-level secretarial position at Roth's Medical and the rigors of school. This left Laurina with the bulk of caring for their brother through his hospitalization and rehab. With little time to devote to working on her craft, she found herself calling in favors from a few acquaintances just to make her bills. One of them suggested that she might try dancing at clubs for a temporary living until Abel got better.

Compared to the meager earnings she received from the occasional small productions she danced in, there was much more money to be had working the "night profession." Between the checks from management and the tips from the customers, not only was she able to save her flat, but she was able to make a dent in her family's mounting bills as well. However, that line of work carried more risk as well. Laurina's talent for dancing easily made her a favorite among the patrons that frequented these seedy establishments, who loved her fluid movements in the skimpy costumes she was compelled to wear.

Unfortunately, after noting her popularity, most club owners wanted her to dole out "special favors" for their more valued and free-spending clientele. Of course, the redhead would have none of that, politely refusing each request. In time, each rebuff would inevitably lead to an ultimatum from the owner, and finally, the abrupt departure of Laurina from that club. It was a perpetual cycle that she would eventually repeat over and over at each new venue.

Then there were the problems with the customers who wanted to "take her home" once her shift was over. The well-meaning ones and those that just had a little too much to drink were easy enough to deal with. A few kind words of assurance, a compliment about their gallantry, and a sweet smile were enough to cause most of them to relent and leave her be. The more insistent and aggressive ones proved to be more of a dilemma, however. Several rough scrapes forced her into taking self-defense courses at the local YWCA, which served her well on more than one occasion, including the time when one bloke actually attempted to rape her.

Fortunately, by using her newfound skills, Laurina escaped unscathed, leaving her assailant lying in a pool of blood on the sidewalk with a bruised groin and a broken nose and jaw. However, the experience had scared her to death. She promptly moved out of her flat in the morning, and then notified her boss that she would not be returning to work. Later that day she found another flat on the opposite side of London.

She would never again work as an exotic dancer. That was five years ago.

Of course, Abel knew nothing about this, and if she could help it, Laurina would make damn sure that he never would.

Yes, simple con work was safer. Much safer.

"Look, we've had this argument time and time again Abel. This is who I am and what I do."

"Yeah, yeah, I know," her brother replied, holding up a hand in surrender.

"I also know you're just trying to protect me, as you've always done. And I appreciate it, love, I do. But I'm a big girl now, and quite capable of taking care of myself."

"I know," he sighed. "I gave up on trying to talk you out of your 'career' a long time ago. I just worry about you Laur, that's all. Life is hard enough without having to worry about whether I'll have to pay your bail to the barristers, or identify your body at the morgue; all because you insist on playing Robin fucking Hood!"

"I'll have you know that my work helped support us all when you were..."

"How many times are you gonna beat me about the head with it Laur?" the big man sighed.

"And how many times are you gonna tell me in so many words that I'm a disappointment to you?" she replied.

His jaw worked a few times as he sought to respond, but realizing the truth in his sister's words, Abel paused, then closed his mouth altogether.

They lapsed into an awkward silence. It happened every time Laurina visited Abel's flat; the same worn out argument, the same protestations, the same reassurances, followed by silence at the end of the dance. It was an emotional ballet that resulted in guilt for her and empty helplessness for him. Granted it hurt less, now that the anger that fuelled their earlier shouting matches had faded over the years. Nevertheless, it still stung.

As if trying to make amends in some small way, Abel made a bit of a show of blowing on his tea, and she watched as swathes of vapor rose from the delicate bone-china cup. Then he lifted the cup and saluted her with a large grin and a nod before taking a sip. She smiled in spite of herself.

He hasn't changed since we were kids. Even when the bloke is being boorishly silly, he comes off as so bloody charming.

"Change of subject," Abel smiled as he fingered the handle of his teacup. "What's so urgent that you had to splash through the puddles to see me?"

"I have news from Galicia."

A shadow passed over the big man's face. "And how is our prodigal baby sister anyway?" he asked sarcastically.

Laurina looked at him slightly hurt. "Now Abel, you know she hasn't done a thing to slight you personally. She's a world away in the States, busy with her nursing project."

Abel returned her look a bit annoyed. "I know. I know. But the old girl didn't even have the good manners to say cheerio before she left. Nor has she bothered to call me, or even send me a bloody text message for god's sake!"

"Abel...."

"At least you get a little news from her when she bothers to remember that she has a family."

"Please," Laurina raised her hands in a pleading gesture. "Forget that for a moment. I need your help."

The big man was about to fire off another retort when he noticed the look of desperation that appeared on her face. His face immediately softened, and his annoyance disappeared.

"What's wrong?"

Laurina set down her teacup and sighed. "I received a letter from her yesterday that seemed quite strange in its tone," she said.

"What does it say?"

"That's the thing; her writing sounds different somehow, and I can't make heads or tails out of it," Laurina replied.

Abel straightened in his rickety chair. "Alright, first thing's first. Perhaps you should start by telling me what exactly our sister has been up to lately. I'm afraid I'm not quite up to speed on that."

"Well, you do remember that she always wanted to become a doctor."

"Quite," Abel nodded, "but the orphanage didn't find it in their coffers to pay for that kind of education. So she became a nurse instead."

"Even so, Galicia never gave up on her dream and she continued to enroll in a variety of advanced medical courses..."

"Which you paid for with your little con jobs," Abel interjected with a laugh.

"Oh stop it you bugger!" Laurina snapped. "It's not that funny."

"You must admit that there is a perverse sort of humor to be found in your extracurricular activities Laur," Abel continued. "I'll never forget how you sold a cement-mixer to a parish priest for building his church annex." The big man replayed the story in his mind and exploded into hearty guffaws. "I'll bet he's probably still waiting for it."

Laurina frowned as he slapped his knee and nearly sloshed his tea in the process. "Abel, I'll have you know that paid for half a year of Galicia's courses!"

"Yes yes, I know. Sorry," he chuckled while wiping tears from his eyes. "I'm just amazed at your talents, old girl. I may not approve of your 'activities,' but that doesn't mean you're not good at it. "

"Well don't go treating it like a joke," the redhead said pointedly. "It helped see her through the rough times, plus I was able to help out the little ones at the Home."

"Paddington's anonymous donor," he replied with a flourish. "At least *they* appreciate it." Abel sobered and shook his head sadly. "That's more than I can say for our baby sister. You constantly go out on a limb for her Laurina, always doing the noble big sister thing, only to have her disappear on us with nary a word. The thought of it still makes me bloody well pissed at her."

"You have no idea about what happened, Abel. Galicia was given a terrific opportunity."

"Oh? What kind of opportunity?"

"To become a doctor."

Abel's jaw dropped.

"Are you serious?"

Seeing his sister nod, he slowly shook his head in wonder. "Well, that's certainly a shocker. Tell me, who offered her this opportunity?"

Laurina sighed and shrugged. "That's the part I'm a bit sketchy about. During her nursing project in Washington D.C., she happened to take a special battery of medical evaluations. When the results came back, this Colonel from the United States Army appeared."

"A Colonel, hmmm?"

"Quite so."

"Indeed," Abel murmured, raising his shaggy eyebrows. After digesting this bit of information for several moments, he leaned back and put down his teacup. "Why in God's name would a high ranking officer of the U.S. Army be interested in Galicia?"

"I don't really know," Laurina admitted.

"Does this Colonel have a name?"

"I think she said his last name was Kern or something like that."

Abel looked Laurina in the eye before slowly shaking his head. "I don't like it. I don't know why, but I don't like it one bit.

"I was also skeptical, but I couldn't get Galicia off of it. It was a chance to finally realize her dream. So she signed an agreement which made her an official contractor for the U.S. Army. A few days later, she was supposed to leave for a military base somewhere in the southwestern United States, but even she didn't know exactly where it was located."

"They must have at least given her a destination airport."

"Yes: Phoenix, Arizona."

"Well, at least that's something. So what exactly is the problem?"

Laurina walked over to the entrance of the flat and pulled an envelope out of an inside pocket of her damp coat and returned to the table. Leaning forward after reclaiming her seat, she waved it back and forth in front of him. "That was six months ago. I'll read you the letter I got from her yesterday, then you'll know."

Abel sat back in his chair and sighed. "Laur, don't be so melodramatic about it. Just read the bloody thing," he said impatiently. Pointedly ignoring his tone, Laurina deliberately lit a cigarette and took a drag. After exhaling a thick cloud of smoke, the redhead unfurled the letter and began to read out loud.

Laur, my "dear" sister,

I only wanted to tell you that I am quite well here. Although the courses are a little boring because they are more about neurology than anatomy and you know how much I hate neurology. At least the food we get in the mess hall is rather good. There is fresh fish available almost every day and the servers have wonderful brown eyes.

After the first quarter, they want to send us to Acapulco for a small vacation, and I'm looking forward to that very much. You remember, don't you, that for us it has always been our little paradise. I'm going to have myself a lobster there first thing and I'm going to open it up with my bare teeth!

So don't worry about your little sister. I have even met somebody here already, a young doctor with green eyes. I must come to an end now. Hugs to you.

Your loving sister,
Galicia

Laurina let the letter sink to her lap. "Well, what do you think?"

While his sister was reading the letter, Abel had allowed his eyes to wander around the apartment. For some unknown reason, they rested on the refuse can under the sink.

"Garbage," he muttered almost to himself. A moment later, he turned his head and looked her in the eye.

"Are you sure this letter is from Gal? Let me see it." He snatched the crumpled paper from Laurina's hands and looked at it thoroughly. "Well, it's quite obviously her handwriting," he mumbled.

"Quite. I'd recognize her messy style anywhere."

Abel nodded. "It's also true that neurology was her best subject. She loved everything about it."

"Glad you noticed," Laurina offered.

Where is he going with this?

"And we also know she didn't like guys with brown eyes." He rolled his eyes. "God knows why."

Laurina snapped her fingers. "There's more to this than meets the eye."

"Yes, a right bit more. I still remember how the three of us used to make fun of the type of sand swept fantasy vacation she mentions here. In Gal's way of thinking, Acapulco means Hell."

"Exactly!" she exclaimed. She paused a moment to think when something pressed against her awareness.

What did Abel say earlier? Ah yes, 'Garbage.' There was something about garbage...

Sudden recognition shone on her face. "Abel, look at that passage about the Lobster."

The big man read and reread the line before shaking his head. "Sorry but I'm stumped on that one."

Laurina took the letter back from him and pointed to the sentence in question. "The lobster is a symbol. It's a hidden message! Remember how we always kept tabs on nurse Garbage at the nursing home?"

Abel pointed a finger at Laurina, recalling the past. "Her name was Harbedge."

"Yes, we called her Garbage. Gal used to go spying in the east wing, and I did it in the west wing. Anytime we discovered something; we'd write a note and deposit our secret message into that tacky porcelain lobster in the main hall."

"Oh? You mean it was hollow?"

Try as she might, Laurina couldn't suppress the grin that appeared unbidden to her face. "Don't tell me you didn't know?" she smiled in mock surprise.

Abel slapped his forehead. "I had no idea. Oh, you wicked little sisters!"

For a moment they laughed heartily while gazing at each other, lost in blissful memories of the past. However, once the letter's implications dawned on them both, they quickly sobered. Abel sat down again and put his teacup aside.

"What does this letter tell you, Laur?"

"This letter states quite clearly that Galicia is not well at all. *And* that she being watched, and therefore had to smuggle a hidden message into her letter. That is why she mentions the lobster she wants to crack open with her bare teeth." Laurina stared intently at her older brother.

"We need to crack the code in her hidden message!"

Abel nodded. "I see. And that's where I come in."

She laid the letter down in front of him. "Abel, you have been interested in cryptography for ages; long before you became a researcher and computer geek, and even when we were back at the Home."

"True enough. However, it's been a long time since I've worked in that field."

"Who cares? I'm sure you haven't lost your deciphering skills. If there is anyone who can break this code, it's you. Please Abel," Laurina pleaded. "I know you're hurt and angry at Galicia for leaving and not contacting you but this is serious. She needs your help."

Abel looked at her for a long moment. Finally, he smiled grimly and shrugged his shoulders in resignation. "Bloody hell woman! You could con the pitchfork from the devil himself, and get it!" A hint of playfulness appeared on his round face as he smiled ruefully. "Well, I suppose I can't very well refuse a challenge like this now can I? Let's take a gander at that letter again, shall we?"

Abel studied the message, while a grateful Laurina stamped out her cigarette in the ashtray, and sat quietly awaiting his verdict. The ticking of the cheap plastic alarm clock on the windowsill became the dominant noise in the kitchen, drowned out occasionally by the bellow of a ship's horn or muffled by the rain drumming against the window panes.

"Hmm," Abel muttered. "Galicia like fantasy novels right?"

"What do you have in mind?"

"Please Laur, humor me and just answer my question."

Laurina knitted her brow, as she tried hard to recall her younger sister's lifestyle.

"Let me think.... she mainly read 'Highlander' tomes...Diana Gabaldon and the like...Irish Folklore. She loved anything Celtic, anything having to do with runes and all that. Bloody boring if you ask me."

"Celtic runes, indeed! Well, look at this, will you..."

He put the letter on the table and pointed towards the top.

"Take a close look at the quotation marks in "dear" Sister.

"And this "o"... It differs from all the others. Basically, it's just a small square."

Abel shifted his 300-pound frame to the left and leaned against the refrigerator. He reached for an open bag of potato chips lying on top and brought them down. Laurina suspected they had probably been lying there open since the night before.

"So what do these symbols suggest?" Abel asked patiently.

"Maybe they are special characters?"

"Bingo! And in fact, it's a specific alphabet! That's why I asked you about her interests, Laur. This small square is a relict from the Tyronic notation, an ancient Irish ampersand, which is still in use today."

"And what exactly are Tyronic notes?" Laurina smiled slyly. "I doubt they have anything to do with music."

"Don't be a twit, Laur. It's Roman shorthand, which is used for text corrections in some parts; in fact, newspaper editors still use it today."

Abel rattled the tea service as he suddenly staggered up from the table. Grimacing with pain, he reached into his pants pocket, pulled out the bottle of Vicodin and shook out two pills. Popping them into his mouth, he washed them down with the last of his tea. "Let me get to my computer. I need to do some programming."

"This won't take too long will it? You know, I have an appointment this evening."

Abel grimaced as he straightened, and shook his head reprovingly at her like a parent would regard a child shunning homework for play. "It'll have to wait," he said. "This is much more important."

"Of course," Laurina acquiesced quietly. "I'll ring up my "date" and tell him I will be late."

"You do that," Abel replied, as he disappeared into the back hallway.

Laurina walked back to the foyer, reached for the cell phone in her coat pocket and pressed a number on speed dial.

"Hello, Mr. Rickenbacker? Yes, this is she. Uh, yes, the weather is rather depressing. Oh no, everything's fine, however, I'm still with a client here. Can we reschedule our appointment by two hours or so? Yes, I have all the proper documents...no, it won't take long, as long as the location, appeals to you. Yes, nine o'clock then...Righty-o, see you then. Cheers!"

Laurina terminated the conversation and sighed, hoping that the time frame she suggested would be enough. Thankfully she heard the clattering of the keyboard from Abel's study showing that he was hard at work on the problem.

Willing herself to relax, Laurina walked over to the grimy window and looked out. The all-day rain had finally stopped, at least for the moment, and a thick fog was beginning to form. As she rested a hand on the windowsill absently, she heard Big Ben tolling seven p.m. Scanning the horizon, she caught sight of the beam of a searchlight tracing arcs in the grey sky like the 20th Century Fox logo she had seen at the beginning of many a movie. She was surprised to find its rhythmic back and forth motion oddly calming.

It always seems like I'm waiting around for something. Waiting for Galicia to grow up and be off on her own, waiting for Abel to recover from his injuries, waiting for a mark to take the bait. Why do I feel like I'm in a holding pattern waiting for my own life to begin? It's like I'm cooped up in a tower waiting for someone to rescue me, like some bloody fairytale princess. What would it be like to be free; to fly like a bird, soaring willy-nilly like that searchlight, with no obligations, no worries, no responsibilities to anyone but me?

She closed her eyes and imagined herself dancing again, pirouetting on a huge stage at the London Ballet. Twirling faster and faster, allowing the world to blur in front of her eyes in a rush of exhilaration. Then she came to rest, standing on point with her arms held aloft like the preening feathers of a red-headed bird, before settling her body to the floor in classic form; all while her adoring audience bathed her in warm applause.

A few wistful moments later, she opened her eyes and allowed the image to fade from her mind as she sighed heavily.

Shit, who am I kidding?

Time passed quickly. Looking up absently at the cheap kitchen clock, Laurina saw that 45 minutes had elapsed since she spoken to Rickenbacker on the phone. Felling a bit antsy, she got up and strolled through the corridor to check on Abel's progress.

Walking down the hallway to his bedroom office, she marveled at how much of the walls were covered with shelves full of books, like a row at the Public Library. Entering the room, Laurina saw Abel sitting at his large "L" shaped oaken desk, hard at work on one of the three open laptops which occupied his "command center." Abel had stopped using desktops – he considered them too immobile. The contradiction made her laugh inside since he was the most sedentary person she had ever known. The one he was currently working on was running a series of calculations; columns of numbers scurrying across the screen, like an image straight out of a Hollywood science fiction. She watched with interest as he pounded the keys, and instantly the columns of numbers changed into diagrams and characters.

Anonymously known online as Killjoy409, he was a fledgling hacker of some notoriety, having defaced the websites of several high profile companies of questionable reputation, as well as the sites of a few politicians. He relished his computer time, especially when he immersed himself in his "virtual world" as he called it; a realm consisting entirely of algorithms, letters, figures, intricate characters and complex calculations.

Glancing at the second laptop, she recognized one of Abel's virtual worlds that he had been so keen about recently. The screen showed the backdrop of the courtyard of a medieval castle where animated characters engaged in warfare, striking each other repeatedly. Next to the main screen was a window where chat messages constantly appeared. Laurina recognized from her earlier visits that behind these animated characters were real players who had decided to meet up in this world to give each other's avatar a thorough bashing. Somehow Abel saw a deeper meaning in this, as he often lost himself in this game world for weeks at a time. At times, he seemed to attach more significance to these online games than to reality itself, but Laurina was always careful not to call him on it.

The third laptop screen revealed another set of calculations, different from the ones on the first screen. This one contained one long column of numbers racing across the screen at breathtaking speed, while a flashing display on the side constantly presented new values.

"What exactly are you doing there?" she asked, casually indicating the third screen.

"Looking for extraterrestrial life," Abel replied just as casually.

"The so-called SETI-Project."

Laurina rolled her eyes and sighed.

"Smashing," she said sarcastically.

Why not? Why wouldn't a computer geek be looking for ET?

"Bloody boring if you ask me," the redhead replied.

"By the way Laur," Abel said, ignoring her comment. "I'm transforming Galicia's text into Tyronic notation; or, to be more precise, into numbers representing the notes. This program displays a graphical representation as soon as a significant pattern arises. You see? Here." He indicated a graph. A letter "L" was already recognizable.

"And you think there is a complete sentence?" Laurina asked anxiously.

"The less you bother me, the sooner we'll know."

"Okay, I'll shut my trap then," she replied chagrined. "Do you have a Coke or a bottle of water or something? I could sure use a drink."

"Check the fridge," he dismissed her with a wave.

Walking back to the kitchen, Laurina opened up the ancient refrigerator. Unfortunately, there was no cold water inside, but she did find a single bottle of Coca-Cola next to an opened bottle of champagne. She could only guess at the story behind this bottle, but looking at it, it seemed clear that his champagne-drinking guest had fled the premises long before the bottle was close to being finished.

Abel probably put her off with his blather about extraterrestrials, his online worlds, and his "Virtual Existence."

Laurina shook her head, picked up the Coke bottle and walked over to the kitchen cupboard. After rummaging through the drawers for an opener and coming up empty, she opened the bottle with the edge of her lighter. She took a long pull directly from the bottle before nervously regarding her watch. It read 8:12 p.m.

For next half hour, she restlessly paced the kitchen. Hopefully, her appointment would wait for her. She was glad that she didn't tell Abel exactly what she had planned for this chap. He probably would have tried to talk her out of it.

"Eureka!"   Electrified by Abel's shout, Laurina bolted back toward his study in a rush. A second later she heard him cry out again. "Bugger me!" Abel stared at the screen in horror as she arrived at his desk. Finally, he looked up at her, and Laurina saw that the color had drained from his face. "Laur," he said hesitantly. "Love, I don't know if you should read this or not."

"You bloody well better get outta my way!" The redhead stepped around the desk until she stood behind him. She gazed at the screen, and recoiled as she read the prominent sentence that stood out in bold letters below the charts:

Forget me. Flee London, they will destroy you. If they catch you trust Kelder.

"Bloody hell!" the beautiful redhead exclaimed anxiously.

So Galicia is in some kind of terrible fix.   And it's nasty enough that she wants me outta the city to boot. But what happened to her, and who are 'They?' And why does she want me to trust Kelder? I'd rather trust a bloody rat! Gal has no idea that the good Inspector would love nothing better than to take me into custody and lock me up in his special cell at the Yard.

Laurina made a decision. There was no way that she could ignore the frightening implications. Something ominous was going on, big enough to threaten her life as well. But Galicia's safety had always been more important to her than her own. She had no choice but to try to save her.

Forget you, Gal? You must be barmy!

Laurina turned on her heels and ran into the kitchen.

"Laur! What are you doing?" Abel exclaimed as he staggered from his seat and limped after her. By the time he reached the flat's entryway Laurina had already donned her coat. He caught sight of the look of determination on her face and immediately knew what it meant.

"You're planning to go after her aren't you?"

"Abel, we have to do something! We need to get to Phoenix Arizona!"

"We?" Abel hesitated. "Well yes, you're right of course. But let's think about it for a moment. It'll be expensive love, especially on such short notice. We'll need cash and lots of it for the plane tickets, somewhere to flop, and hell we may even have to bribe someone."

"That's why I can't miss my date!"

Recognition came into Abel's mind.

"So it really is another con, is it? And I'll bet it's a right profitable one at that. Laurina, what exactly are you planning?" When the redhead didn't answer right away, he sighed heavily.

"Please, love don't do this, not again."

"We don't have a choice, Abel. It's the only way." She clutched one of his large hands and held it tenderly. "Don't worry. I won't do anything stupid, I promise.

Wait here until I get back, please. I promise I'll contact you the minute I'm finished, and we'll make plans to leave for America."

"But Laur, we'll need a plan of action!"

"That's where you come in Abel. Work out a plan, and we'll figure out the details once we're on the plane."

She quickly made her way to the door preparing to depart.

"What if something happens and you get hurt or worse?" he said sadly as he walked up behind her. "I don't think I could bear it."

Laurina paused briefly at the door and looked at the big man. Lines of worry creased the center of his brow like a washboard.

Oh, Abel. You're always looking out for my welfare. You're the best brother a girl could ever have!

She lightly touched his cheek with her right hand. "It'll be okay Abel. You'll see. Now buck up you bugger and wish me luck!"

Abel swallowed the large lump growing in his throat. Then impulsively, he pulled the redhead close, kissed her on the cheek and hugged her tightly. Reaching into a caddy next to the door, he pulled out a small red umbrella and pressed it into her hands.

"Here Laur, take it. It'll stave off the worst of the rain. I'll contact Clarence at home and take a leave of absence. He won't be happy about it, but if I tell him it's a family matter, he won't say much. In the meantime, you mind your step! I have an awful feeling about this whole bloody affair and I'll feel a damned sight better once you finish this caper of yours. Call me the minute you're out of harm's way, and we'll meet up. And please, do be careful!"

Chapter 2

The deep, resonating sound of a foghorn moaned its sad call over the nearby docks. Once again, rain fell ever so softly from the sky and seemed to add to the eerie mist that curled its way through the dark streets of London's harbor district. A dark warehouse stood prominently among a cluster of smaller buildings, keeping its solitary vigil over the Shipyard. The cavernous building was mostly barren inside save for the piles of discarded shipping crates and related debris that surrounded its edges. That and a large steel work table which sat in the center of the floor. Along one wall, a metal stairway ascended to an open maintenance catwalk that ran along both walls with one section that led to the lone upstairs office.

A large girder was suspended along the center of the ceiling, framed by the smaller ones which ran along both sides, curving down the walls to the floor, giving anyone who stepped inside the impression that they had been swallowed by a great metal whale. Attached to the center girder was a crane that was still in good working condition; perfect for moving crates of cargo to be shipped. Several thick linked chains dangled from the apparatus, and a hint of tinkling echoed through the warehouse as a slight breeze from the open windows above stirred them slowly to life.

The rain outside, though light, seemed to beat thunderously against the metal roof of the warehouse. Through the dirt-streaked glass, two figures could be seen in quiet conversation next to the work table.

The young woman was the taller of the two. The full-length black leather coat she wore seemed too large for her frame and gave her the appearance of a little girl playing dress-up with her daddy's clothes. However, the small black leather mini skirt and black fishnet stockings underneath revealed her to be all woman. A closer look showed that the red silk blouse she wore was only partially tucked into her skirt, and her long shapely legs fell away into tall black leather boots. Her companion stood next to her nervously clutching a grey metal briefcase against his chest as if it were a life preserver. He was a short, plump, balding man in his late forties embodying the stereotypical British businessman; soft, well mannered and well fed. He wore the usual natty brown tweed suit and vest, as well as a white silk ascot which he thought gave his appearance a bit of dash. However, any hint of the debonair was quickly dispelled by the thick round horned rimmed spectacles the man wore on his plump oval face and the continuous nervous sweat that appeared on his brow.

Poor bloke looks like a myopic egg.

The woman waited patiently as the man excused himself and reached into his jacket. Producing a tan silk handkerchief with a flourish, he proceeded to pat it delicately across his sweaty forehead. Finished, he tucked the cloth back into his vest pocket while still clutching the briefcase to his chest. Clearing his throat he smiled with a bit of embarrassment.

"Sorry about that Miss Thompson. Please go on."

"I'm quite sure that this location will suit all of your requirements Mr. Rickenbacker," Laurina Hawks continued, lifting her hands to indicate her surroundings. She recited the order back to him. "Medium-sized riverfront warehouse, two-thousand square meters in volume, separate electrical shack with a backup generator in good working order, 3 one hundred meter berths and a loading ramp complete with access to the bay. It's even got a nice private office for you to boot." She smiled at the egg-man with confidence.

"Im-p-p-pressive," Harvey Rickenbacker stammered anxiously. "And the price, w-what a bargain. H-How did you come b-by this property so cheaply?"

The redhead continued to smile winningly at him, even though the man's stuttering was getting on her nerves. "Well," she began, "my clients are quite resourceful, and shrewd bargainers. They seek out properties with potential like this one and strike while the iron is hot. Then they seek out certain uh...'discriminating' customers like yourself who recognize a bargain when they see one and make an offer. By offering to help them avoid certain odious surcharges by dealing only in cash, my clients are able to offer properties at a substantial discount."

"Indeed, I under-s-s-stand completely," the plump man nodded vigorously, speaking in a conspiratorial tone. "The Crown's taxes for businesses can be quite, er excessive."

Taking a breath, he made his decision. "I will accept your terms, Miss Thompson, provided that the wording of deed of sale is in order. If you have the d-d-document with you, I'll give it a thorough going over now." He extended his chubby hand her way, grasping at the empty air like a child begging for candy.

"I do indeed," Laurina replied, holding a slim palm up to his face. "You do have the funds I trust?"

"Oh! Y-y-yes," he stammered while flushing with embarrassment. He shakily laid the grey briefcase on the steel table next to the woman's red umbrella and clicked the latches open with a snap. Multiple images of the Queen smiled back at the young woman as she gazed lovingly at the large stacks of bank notes.   He giggled a bit before speaking again.

"Sorry, but I feel a bit like one of those ballsy drug lords they show on the telly. Nasty buggers. Well then, here's the 250,000 pounds sterling as agreed Miss Thompson. Would you like to verify the contents?"

A slight frown appeared on the woman's face before quickly vanishing; hastily replaced by a small smile of professionalism. Somehow, even hearing this egg man refer to her by her chosen alias irritated her immensely. "That is not necessary Mr. Rickenbacker. Your reputation as a trustworthy businessman precedes you, but please, just call me Nancy," she replied, smiling sweetly.

Reaching into the folds of her trench coat, she produced a large manila envelope. She withdrew a document made of thick parchment paper from inside and placed it on the table for his inspection. Rickenbacker picked it up and noted its weight. His eyes then carefully scanned the parchment looking for any abnormalities. He also verbalized each word in a low prim and proper voice as he read, hoping that his ear would catch what his eyes did not.

The closer he came to the end of the document, the more excited his voice became. His palms became even sweatier, and the paper began to rattle as it shook within his hands. By the time he reached the bottom, a smile of triumph emerged on his round face. The language of the document was correct, the certificate was signed in all the appropriate places, and yes, the official gold foil seal stood out like an exclamation on the right bottom corner. Everything seemed to be in order. He couldn't believe his good fortune. The Dover property was finally his, and at a bargain price to boot!

"Then it's a deal?" she asked sweetly.

"Certainly," Rickenbacker replied excitedly.

Laurina reached forward to shake his sweaty hand. Finishing the handshake with a nod, the chubby man made a flourish with his right hand inviting her to take the money. The slim woman nodded with a smile, snapped the lid of the briefcase shut and lifted it from the table, while he folded up and placed the deed to the Dover Shipyards into an inner jacket pocket.

A sudden scraping noise drew their attention to the east side of the warehouse. The gritty sound of booted footfalls echoed loudly on the concrete walk outside, while at the same time an authoritative voice could be heard speaking loudly through a megaphone.

"Laurina Hawks, you are under arrest for crimes against the Crown! Come out with your hands where we can see them!"

"Bloody fuzz. Shit!" Laurina murmured under her breath.

Not now! Not when I've just scored this deal, and I'm this close to meeting up with Abel and going after Galicia. Interference from the Bizzies is the last thing I need.

"W-w-what are they t-t-talking about?" Harvey Rickenbacker stuttered. "Who is this Hawks person they're referring to?"

Laurina ignored the egg man as she reached into her coat and produced a leather strap which she clipped onto the handle of the case. Once secured, she looped it over her opposite shoulder. "Mr. Rickenbacker," she turned and bade him farewell with a formal bow.

The nervous man blinked with astonishment as the woman rushed past him and darted up the metal stairs, as a group of constables burst into the warehouse, followed by a tall man in civilian clothes. The men hesitated slightly as they caught sight of the beautiful woman in fishnet stockings and miniskirt bounding upstairs.

"Don't even rest there you dolts! Go after her!" the tall man shouted with frustration.

As he spoke, Laurina reached the landing of the catwalk, turned, and continued running toward the office at the opposite corner of the warehouse. The air vibrated with the hollow echoes of the heavy footfalls as five of the men pursued the con artist, taking the stairs two at a time to gain ground on her. Several of the constables headed back outside of the large building to cut off any potential external escape route, while their fellows upstairs pursued the woman. Each man secretly hoped against hope that they would capture the Hawks woman before she could elude them once again, and thereby avoid another tongue lashing or worse from their superior.

Laurina flung open the door of the darkened office, ducked inside, and quickly locked it behind her. After propping a chair back against the doorknob, she rushed over to her predetermined exit, a wooden door beside the manager's desk which opened outside to a fire escape which overlooked the docks. She carefully glanced outside, looking for signs of pursuit. Judging that the coast was clear, the redhead slipped outside just as her pursuers crashed against the locked door. Grabbing hold of the railing, the beautiful redhead raced down the stairs as quietly as possible. Reaching the landing, she ignored the rusty extension ladder to the ground, clambering over the railing instead, and dropped onto a large ancient cargo container long abandoned by its previous owners.

One of the officers, alerted by the sound, rounded the corner at a full run, hoping to be the one lucky enough to catch her. What he caught instead was a booted foot from above that landed flush against his face, breaking his nose and knocking his head backward. The force of the blow, coupled with his forward momentum, knocked the man off his feet, flipping him end over end until he landed face first into a large puddle of mud. The hapless officer gurgled in pain as he extracted his face from the muck long enough to catch a breath. Dazed by the impact of the blow, he was barely conscious enough to catch sight of a lone figure jumping onto the wet ground and swiftly making its way into the concealing fog.

Inside the warehouse, someone else was also enveloped in a fog of sorts.

"W-w-w-what happened? What's going on?" demanded a flustered Rickenbacker in a shaky voice amid the chaos of uniformed men running to and fro.

He watched with dread as one of the officers came back inside the warehouse, hastily making his way toward the tall, slightly rumpled figure in a worn trench coat and an aged tweed hat; a commanding presence who stood nearby. Behind him, two other policemen were carrying in one of their own, covered in mud with a bloodied face. After a short discussion, the face of the tall man reddened, and after several terse words, the messenger quickly backed away from him in fear. Shaking with rage, tweed hat quickly regained his composure, and marched over to the little round man, producing a pair of handcuffs in a scarred right hand.

"I'm Inspector Richard Kelder," he began, before spitting a gnawed toothpick from his thin mouth. "And by order of the Crown, you Harvey Rickenbacker are under arrest for business fraud and evasion of taxes."

He spun the rotund suspect easily and quickly cuffed his wrists behind his back. Before the shaken man could protest, the Inspector leaned down and whispered grimly, "Sorry to inform you guv, but on top of everything else, you've been scammed. This is the third property that this little lady has "sold" without ownership or authorization this year, and with her on the run, it looks like she left you up the bloomin' creek without a paddle."

The blood drained from the portly man's face. His fleshy lips pursed like a fish. "T-t-this cannot be," he said in a quivering voice, nodding toward his heart. "I've got the original deed for the property from Miss Thompson here in my breast pocket."

"Nancy Thompson, incidentally, is just one of several aliases that our Miss Hawks uses to scam unsuspecting blokes like you. May I?" Kelder asked, reaching into the fold of Rickenbacker's coat without waiting for a response. The tall Inspector's eyes squinted as he quickly scanned the document with an expert's detachment.

"It's almost perfect to be sure, but as I suspected, definitely forged," he pronounced with finality while pointing to a flaw only his trained eyes could see.

"Unfortunately for you, Laurina Hawks just happens to be one of the best document forgers in all of London. Poor bugger. Your greed bought you nothing but a beautiful piece of paper and a trip down to Scotland Yard."

Harvey Rickenbacker's mind whirled as the reality of the situation came crashing down on him like a lead weight, but not because he was worried about doing any jail time. His barristers could get him out of that easily, or at least keep the courts tied up indefinitely. It was the thought of his professional reputation being tarnished that made him suffer the most. He considered himself to be a wise and savvy businessman who watched dispassionately, while many of his contemporaries had been fooled into bad deals. And oh, had he needled them for it.

"T-t-tough break there, chap" he would say while clicking his tongue condescendingly. "It could happen to anyone."

The words while soothing on the outside would always hold the mocking undertone of, "But of course never to me." Over the years many of his contemporaries had chafed under his smugness, and now, because of his own greed, it has come back to haunt him. Now, with this terrible turn of events, Rickenbacker had lost more money than all of them put together, frittering away 250,000 pounds sterling with absolutely nothing to show for it. What grated on him, even more, was the fact that he had lost it due to the charms of a woman!

"I still can't believe it!" the fleshy man exclaimed. "She knew all the right things to say, down to the proper business terminology!"

The Inspector nodded. "Quite. She knows her craft, I'll give 'er that. As I said, you're not the only one Hawks has deceived. There have been a number of these "occurrences" over the last five years or so."

What he didn't tell Rickenbacher was that Metropolitan Police Service suspected that a large portion of the funds from these confidence games ended up being laundered and then deposited into the coffers of various charities scattered across London, including one in particular: Paddington Foundling Home; the orphanage that Laurina Hawks grew up in. Unfortunately, due to lack of evidence, they couldn't move on the charities themselves. Until she becomes careless, or someone makes a mistake, they had no choice but bide their time.

The egg man remained silent as he considered his current position. He would most certainly be removed from the company and shown the door of course, but not before there was a hearing in front of his own board of directors. There he would be a made a laughingstock in front of the same group of men he had passively ridiculed. Worse still was the fact that once word of this embarrassment got out into the business community, he wouldn't be able to get a job anywhere; not even as a lowly clerk. He might even be held personally liable for the loss and compelled to repay it himself, out of his own holdings. His career and his life were ruined.

The shock of this realization caused Rickenbacker's stomach to lurch sickeningly, as his vision began to darken. The hapless man wobbled a bit before finding himself in the grasp of the rumpled Inspector, who guided his slumping form safely onto a nearby chair. He shook his head ruefully.

"This just can't be," he muttered. "She was too bloody pretty to be a con artist."

Kelder chuckled at this line.

"Pretty yes, but make no mistake, she's a sly one she is, and dangerous. The last officer who tried to bring her in on his own ended up missing. We found him the next morning in a daze, wandering the streets stark naked, with two broken arms."

"W-w-wha..." stuttered the wide-eyed victim.

"W-w-wha indeed," mocked Inspector Kelder.

He stuck the tip of his pencil to his tongue and began to jot down notes.

"Now let's start at the beginning my dear Mr. Rickenbacker," he asked in a businesslike tone, as he began to formally interview the latest victim. "When did you first come in contact with Miss...Thompson?" Kelder added with a smirk.

Chapter 3

Laurina continued to race through thickening fog. Knowing these alleys from childhood, she instinctively ducked right and left to confuse any pursuit, careful to run quietly on the grimy wet cobblestones. Minutes later, satisfied that she had lost any of the Constables that may have been chasing her, the redhead emerged onto a main street and slowed her pace to an easy walk, so as not to draw undue attention. A light but steady rain was falling in earnest, and the young Brit cursed her inattentiveness as she remembered that the umbrella she had borrowed from Abel was still lying on the table inside the Dover shipyard, almost certainly in police custody by now. She absently buttoned up her trench coat while casting furtive glances all around. She was so consumed with watching for foot pursuit that she barely paid attention to the sound of the engine of the dark sedan that started up behind her.

Alone in her thoughts, she continued down the sidewalk as the shadowy vehicle slowly pulled away from the deli where it had been parked, creeping its way forward to the intersection before coming to a stop. Its wiper blades swept across the windshield like the finger of a hunter wiping away brow sweat before taking aim, flicking the moisture left and right. Inside, the glow of a burning cigarette lit half of a man's face before dimming as the driver inhaled. His passenger having finished his own smoke rolled down the window and tossed the butt out into the wet night.

As the ember of his cigarette died, he reached into his jacket, pulled out an odd looking handgun, and loaded it with a tranquilizer dart. Aiming it at the young woman, he waited for a clear shot. Nine meters ahead, a sizable gap appeared between two parked cars; more than enough room to do the job. Like a shark, the dark vehicle slowly but steadily accelerated as driver and gunman prepared to strike.

Suddenly a bright golden flash lit up the interior of the vehicle, momentarily blinding them. This was followed by two gasps of surprise and pain as something struck their heads with a dull thud. The passenger slumped sideways into the leg and arm of the unconscious driver, inadvertently turning the steering wheel toward the left. The car picked up speed until it lurched over the curb with a sickening scrape of metal and concrete, and gained the sidewalk, hurtling towards the young Brit.

Laurina Hawks turned at the sound and gasped in horror at the sight of the speeding sedan two meters away bearing down on her. Just before the moment of impact, she screamed, throwing her arms in front of her reflexively as she caught a glimpse of her own reflection in the windshield glass. Oddly, time seemed to slow and the air about her became thick as syrup as she closed her eyes to the inevitable. At the same time, she could clearly smell the briny odor of the fog's moisture, the burning oil of exhaust fumes, and the nicotine from a dying cloud of cigarette smoke.

The golden flash knocked the breath out of her body as the dark sedan struck, mercilessly launching her backward into the air. Like molten honey, the energy covered her, surrounding her form like an aura. Laurina's eyes snapped open just as her back and head slammed into the wall of Molly's Bakery, followed by the car's crushing metal embrace around her chest. Light flashes exploded in her brain by the impact and she felt her lungs suddenly collapse from the pressure of the vehicle, but oddly there was no pain. As shock caused her brain to shut down into unconsciousness, her eyes widened for just an instant as the vehicle, the sidewalk and the entire wet night itself winked into pixilated fragments before finally dissolving into darkness.

Semi-consciousness and pain sprouted into sudden clarity and horror as the two men in the vehicle caught sight of their quarry pinned between their car and the building.   Quickly forcing their doors open, they stumbled onto the sidewalk toward the trapped woman, still shaken from the crash. Both stared in amazement at the sight.   The sedan's front end was totally demolished, with the center grille crumpled back a meter from the impact with the woman, while the rest of it had hugged itself around her body. Wisps of steam escaped into the air like fleeing ghosts blending into the fog, as drops of hot water from the wrecked radiator sizzled onto the cool wet sidewalk. While the vehicle's damage was extensive, strangely enough, there was no blood visible on the woman's clothing or from her mouth, which would normally be expected from such an impact.

"Bugger me!" one of the men groaned. "We'll be raked over the coals for this!"

The faint but growing sound of a siren echoed in the distance.

"We're dead," his shorter companion cried in anguish.

"No, it's not our fault. Someone interfered with the job."

"An' there's no time to clean up this bloody mess either. Lids'll be crawlin' all over it"

"Quit whinin' like a bloomin' frilly and grab her case for the boss. HQ will have to handle the rest of it."

Complying with his partner, the smaller man picked up the grey briefcase lying on the hood of the vehicle where it had landed during the impact and checked the latches to make sure they were still secure. Satisfied, the pair turned away from the body of Laurina Hawks. Concealing their faces as they moved, the two men fled from the wreckage as the warble of the siren grew louder. Thanks to their training, their booted footfalls barely made a sound on the gritty wet sidewalk, as they melted into the growing fog.

Drops of spittle flew into the air as an angry voice spoke into a hand communicator.

"What do you mean you don't have her? What happened?"

Using every ounce of self-control he possessed, the broad-shouldered man calmed himself and listened patiently to his subordinate's report. Breathing heavily, his nostrils flared as he took in each detail. As the moments passed, a vein grew more pronounced along the side of his skull, worming its way toward his furrowed brow. Still, the man in power managed to hold his sizable anger in check. When the caller finally finished his explanation, he waited silently, allowing the growing tension to build between them. He continued to wait until the sound of a nervous swallow could be heard over the comm.

"Report to my office with the briefcase the moment you two return," he ordered tightly.

"Yes sir!" a relieved sigh escaped into the transmission.

Click!

The boss slammed a large hand against the massive oaken desk that dominated his office, sweeping everything except the office intercom toward the nearest wall. The piston in the heavy leather chair hissed in protest as he settled his weight on it, while his broad shoulders slumped at the same time, giving the impression that his whole body was deflating. Certainly, he felt that way. Who would have thought that a simple operation like this one could get so botched up? Each and every move was set up carefully to advance his future plans. All he needed was the Hawks bitch and everything would have gone like clockwork.

Now everything has gone to shit!

And what was this report about someone or something interfering with the operation? Did she have an accomplice? No. She always worked alone. His subordinate probably made up the story as an excuse for his bungling.

"Incompetent fools! All they had to do was tranq her!" he roared into the empty air.

The sound of scraping feet could be heard just outside the office door, but after hearing his outburst, no one would dare enter. Leaning forward, the man buried his head in his hands.

"I was so close! The gods must delight in cursing me," he sighed. A sudden buzzing from the intercom jolted him out of his dark thoughts. It was followed immediately by an urgent voice.

"Sir, an unauthorized intrusion into the Interface appeared on our board just moments ago."

"Is it from the Sempai?" he asked, suddenly ramrod straight in his seat.

"No sir," the voice continued. "What is strange is that this incursion seems to have somehow originated from *outside*."

From outside? How could that be? That's impossible.

Unless…

"Listen to me very carefully Doctor," he said urgently. "It's her! I don't know how, but it's got to be. Set up a perimeter around that sector immediately. Once it's established, send in a retrieval unit. Assign it to someone who won't screw it up this time!"

"Consider it done sir!" the voice replied smartly, before breaking the link.

A predatory smile slowly crawled across the broad man's face. Perhaps the gods haven't cursed him after all.

The blare of a honking car horn followed by indeterminable shouting woke her with a start. Laurina blinked her eyes several times, adjusting them to the light before moving. Looking around slowly, she caught sight of a line of buildings facing each other, with several garbage cans and a dumpster brimming with refuse resting along their walls. The bricked structure closest to her displayed a rough metal door with the words, "service entrance" scrawled in white paint at the top. Gathering her strength, Laurina crawled over to it, and twisted herself into a sitting position, leaning against the cool red bricks. It was evening, but the light from the many street lamps, storefronts, and cars in the area lit up the night like the sun. The noise coming from the alley entrance was a cacophony of sound that bombarded her ears like salvos from a gunship. She felt groggy and was trying hard to regain her bearings. She looked down the other end of the alley and saw huge buildings looming over her, brightly lit from ground to apex. The slow blinking red lights at their tops gave a true indication of just how massive they were.

This is definitely not London.

Laurina climbed unsteadily to her feet and took a shaky step towards the brightly lit thoroughfare. A sudden realization made itself known, and Laurina feverishly touched her arms, and her chest, tracing the lines of her body searching for any signs of damage, but there were none.

That bloomin' car hit me straight on, I know it! Somehow I'm not dead or hurt. But what happened to it?

Her heart fluttered anxiously as another thought entered her awareness.
The briefcase!
She searched every inch of the alley, including the dumpsters and every disgusting pile of debris nearby, desperately hoping to find the money she had acquired from Rickenbacker. The search was fruitless. The case of money had disappeared along with the car. Not even one banknote was left behind.

Oh no! All my money's gone! What the fuck am I supposed to do now?

Realizing she couldn't remain where she was for much longer, Laurina reassessed her physical condition before moving on. Other than the disorientation in her head, which was slowly passing away, she was a bit ruffled but otherwise no worse for wear. The redhead brushed a few smudges of dirt from her coat, and after taking several shaky steps, she emerged from the alley onto the main thoroughfare. She gasped involuntarily as she took in her surroundings.
There were throngs of people everywhere. They filled both sidewalks; some moving quickly with

purpose while others strolled at a more leisurely pace. She spotted families of tourists walking in small groups with cameras in hand, smartly dressed businessmen and women chatting on cell phones, and crisply uniformed delivery people emerging from panel trucks on both sides of the street carrying packages to their appointed destinations. A young man with spiked blonde hair wearing mismatched clothing adorned with chains strode past her, carrying a large boom-box on his shoulder. Punk rock at ear-splitting decibels blared into the crowd, prompting looks of annoyance from those he passed.

Occasionally Laurina would catch sight of street people shambling down the edge of the sidewalk, who seemed to travel in their own bubble. The crowd of passersby sidestepped around the homeless folk, paying them little attention as they attended to their own purposes. The bravest of these unfortunates held out their hands for any help that might be offered, but more often than not, they were ignored. One of them, an elderly woman in a tattered brown coat passed her by, muttering unintelligibly to herself with a glazed look in her eyes. In her wake, the combined stench of urine and body odor emanating from her nearly knocked Laurina over. Holding a free hand over her nose, the Brit watched as the woman disappeared into the steam that rose from one of the manhole covers that occasionally dotted the gritty sidewalk. Nearby, a yellow taxi screeched to a halt and honked loudly as another of the destitute blundered in front of it.

"Hey ya homeless bastard! Get the fuck outta the road!" a muscular black cab driver yelled at the shabby form as he passed, before accelerating forward in indignation.

Laurina looked at the cab carefully as it took off and was startled when she realized it was driving on the wrong side of the street. In fact, all the cars were! In her confusion, she noticed a beefy middle-aged man heading in her direction. He wore a yellow hard hat, a stained tee shirt partially covered by an orange safety vest, and a massive tool belt that straddled his ample belly and faded blue jeans. Drawing up her courage, she stepped in front of the construction worker, blocking his advance.

"Beg your pardon," Laurina asked softly. "Can you tell me where I am?"

"Damn crack addict," the man muttered in disgust.

Scanning her figure he softened a bit.

"Yer in Brooklyn lady," he said in a distinctly New York accent.

Reaching into a pocket, he pulled out a ten dollar bill and handed it to her.

"He-yah. Go get some food. A pretty girl like you shouldn't be hangin' around these streets alone."

Laurina's eyes widened in shock. "What? I'm where?"

The man's face hardened again as if he had never seen her before.

"Damn crack addict!" the man muttered in disgust. "Yer in Brooklyn lady."

His face softened and once again, reaching into a pocket, he pulled out a ten dollar bill and handed it to her.

"He-yah. Go get some food. A pretty girl like you shouldn't be hangin' around these streets alone."

Frozen in bewilderment, Laurina's mouth moved but no words come out. Once again the construction worker spoke unbidden.

"Damn crack addict!" the man said in disgust. "You're in Brooklyn lady."

For the third time, the man pulled out a ten dollar bill and handed it to her.

"He-yah. Go get some food. A pretty girl like you shouldn't be hangin' around these streets alone."

Instantly the man disappeared in front of her only to reappear a half block down the sidewalk, still saying the same line. Seconds later, the same yellow cab screeched on the road in ahead of her, and barely avoided the same homeless person she had seen earlier.

"Hey, ya homeless bastard! Get the fuck outta the road!" the very same cab driver yelled before continuing on down the street with a screech of tires.

Laurina's jaw dropped in astonishment, and she noticed her right eye began to twitch uncontrollably.

Bugger me! I must've taken a blow to the head or something...or I'm still dreaming. Either way, it's like I've woken up as Alice in Wonderland!

Obviously, something was very wrong. There was no telling how much time had passed, but it became painfully clear to Laurina that she was definitely not in London, or at least not the London she knew. She ambled numbly down the sidewalk, occasionally bumping into people as she passed. Thankfully no one confronted her about her inattentiveness, choosing instead to scowl at her before moving on. Eventually, the Brit wandered into a more open area, and in the distance, she could see the tall iconic steel structure that loomed over the riverfront. She instantly recognized it from photos she'd seen in magazines. The Brooklyn Bridge!

Alright. I'm in America. Or something in the like. But how the hell did I end up in Brooklyn of all places? The last thing I remember was that car... in London! What the hell is going on here?

Thoughts raced through her mind like vapors in the wind. She could barely grasp them before they would disappear. Did she dream it all? No. This was no dream. Somehow she not only survived a head-on collision with a vehicle, but someone or something had moved her from London to Brooklyn. But how? Why? So many questions! By some crazy twist of fate, she was now wandering the streets of New York alone, with nothing but thirty American dollars at her disposal.

Trying to take stock of her situation, Laurina pulled her trench coat tighter around her body, trying as much to shield herself from madness as from the chill of the evening.

Weary and frustrated, she sat on the street curb and started to weep. She was so confused. While attempting to make sense of things, she caught a whiff of prepared food floating in the light breeze, and her stomach began to rumble. How long had it been since she had last eaten? Looking to the left she saw a small silver building that looked like a railroad car with rounded edges squatting among the larger structures nearby. She recognized it from movies she had seen as an American diner. Remembering the bills folded up in her coat pocket she made a decision. Half-heartedly she stood up, wiped the tears from her face, walked across the street and stepped through the door of the diner into the coffee-tinged warmth inside. A smattering of people sat in booths or at tables talking in muted tones to one another. She scanned the interior while at the same time avoiding eye contact. Thankfully, no one paid her much attention as she slipped into an empty booth in the back corner.

"What'll it be Miss?" asked a plump woman in a pink apron.

She flipped open her pad to take her order.

"Just coffee, for now, thank you." smiled the young redhead absently. "Oh, and a Danish."

The waitress snapped her pad closed and gave Laurina an irritated look before moving away. In seconds she produced a steaming hot cup of coffee and a plate holding a cheese Danish and placed them on the table. The young woman wrapped her hands around the thick white mug taking in its comforting aroma. She took a small sip and felt the warmth of the dark liquid chase away the chill of the air outside. As she took a second sip, she noticed the large waitress still standing in front of her staring expectantly.

"Sorry." Laurina smiled sheepishly, as she reached into her coat pocket and pulled out a ten dollar bill from her meager stash of American money.

The large woman grabbed it from her hand and turned to the cash register. She reappeared a moment later and unceremoniously dumped a pile of limp bills and change on the plastic tabletop, causing one of the coins to spin like a dervish. After the server left, the young Brit freed a spoon from the napkin it was wrapped in, poured a heap of sugar from the nearby glass shaker, and slowly stirred sweetness into the hot brew. Taking a sip, she smiled grimly and lost herself in the cup.

Thank God for the simplicity of a good cup of coffee.

She quickly devoured the flaky pastry while pondering her next move. As she was swallowing the last bite, the waitress returned with the same irritated look on her face. Producing a second cup of coffee and danish, she set them on the tabletop in front of the startled young woman, grabbed several bills from the table, and walked away.

With a groan, Laurina watched helplessly as the waitress came back with a third steaming cup along with another pastry, and grabbed more change from the table. She couldn't help but feel lost. Her head hurt. Pressure pounded the back of her eyes and she put the coffee cup down to rub her temples. Moments later, the plump woman came back with another mug and plate in her hands and grabbed more money. She looked at the waitress and just shook her head.

No, this isn't Wonderland. This is insanity! It's like I've blundered into the friggin' Twilight Zone!

A sudden thought struck her like a thunderbolt.

Abel! If I'm here in New York, perhaps he made it as well. He might even be looking for me right now!

Her heart was awash with hope as she quickly reached into the inner breast pocket of her coat. Feeling the emptiness there, hope suddenly changed to a feeling of anxiety, as she rummaged through the rest of her pockets. Finally, anxiety gave way to dread as she came up empty-handed.

Her cell phone was missing!

Bugger!

As she contemplated this newest development, something tugged at her awareness, and out of the corner of her eye, Laurina noticed a dark shape moving outside of her window. Sensing danger, she turned to see a black sedan pulling up in front of the diner. It looked like the same vehicle that slammed into her on the streets of London. She watched with dismay as both front doors opened in unison and two men in dark suits emerged. The right rear door opened as well and a third man stepped out onto the curb. They had the blank nondescript look that reeked of London's Criminal Investigation Department.

Oh great, just what I need.

The three men turned and walked purposefully towards the diner. In a panic, Laurina slid out of her booth and quickly made her way to the woman's restroom in the rear of the structure.

Once inside, she quietly opened the door a crack and watched as the newcomers walked up to the counter. The man in the lead confronted the round waitress and spoke pointedly to her. The color seemed to drain out of the large woman's face, and she pointed a hammy arm to the booth in the corner that she had vacated.

Shit!

Allowing the door to close behind her, the young Brit looked around the bathroom and spied a narrow window that faced a long alleyway. Fortunately, it was not locked and opened easily. Like a cat, she slid quickly out the narrow gap and landed lightly on the concrete below. No sooner had she hit the ground when a man's face appeared in the window. The face retreated a moment only to be replaced by a hand wielding a gun.

She bolted down the dark alley dodging from side to side, as several shots rang out. Something like glass or plastic bit into the old building on her right side, throwing sharp fragments against the side of her head along with a splash of some type of liquid with a heavy medicinal tang. Looking down, she saw a smashed cylinder with a bent and broken tip lying on the littered ground like a dead mosquito.

Tranquilizer dart?

Her mind reeled as she threw up her arms reflexively, and continued to run toward the end of the alley.

Why are these men shooting tranqs at me? They're not trying to kill me. They're trying to knock me out. Were they sent by Rickenbacker?

The shots subsided but as the redhead turned to look back, she saw the other two men pursuing her at a rapid pace. Laurina ran faster than she ever had before. Her legs burned as she jumped over trashcans and splashed through dank pools of water. Arriving at an L shaped junction, she rounded the corner and came face to face with the side of a large building. She had reached a dead end! Searching desperately, she saw no way out and nothing to aid her defense. She could see a fire escape looming above, but it was folded up and there was no way to reach it. Anxiously, Laurina glanced back to the alley's junction, waiting for her pursuers to round the corner.

Jump!

Something screamed inside her head. She looked up at the building again. It seemed to be fifteen or twenty stories high.

Jump! The thought came again.

Maybe if I get a running start I can reach the fire escape.

JUMP!

Laurina took a few steps backward, crouched down and leaped up with all her might. Suddenly a spasm-like electric pulse shook her body. As her muscled propelled her upward, she watched with astonishment as the fire escape ladder zoomed past, and she continued to rise high into the air.

What the fuck?

The young woman's leap carried her to the top of the building. Her arms and legs swung wildly as she cleared the edge, and as her feet made contact, she stumbled awkwardly and fell onto the tar-papered roof, rolling two-thirds of its width before coming to an abrupt stop. Lying face down on the gritty surface, Laurina noticed that while she had landed quite heavily, there was no pain. The feeling of electricity that had charged her legs spread throughout her body with a warm rush, deadening the impact. She felt her skin tingling as if it was being scrubbed hard with a loofah sponge, and a sudden feeling of euphoria began to take hold of her.

How the hell did I get up here? What's going on?

Catching her breath, she pulled herself to her feet and managed to stumble forward a few meters, when a loud airy whine and thud caught her attention from behind. She turned to find one of the men who had been chasing her standing at the rooftop's edge. A moment later, he was joined by his companions, who landed knees bent with relative ease, a brief hiss of air emanating from their footwear.

Bloody hell!

The young Brit dashed to the end of the roof. Once again, the voice in her head prompted her to jump, and this time she didn't hesitate. She leaped over the edge, making for the rooftop of a building below her. She landed on her feet this time and continued to run hard and fast. She approached the building's edge and saw that the next one was taller and a considerable distance away, separated by the traffic of a busy street. Without stopping to think about what she was doing, Laurina jumped high into the air, propelling herself across the wide gap and onto the next rooftop. The sound of several impacts from behind told her she had not escaped yet. She continued along the tall roof searching for her next destination as she ran. Faster and faster Laurina ran until she reached the edge of the roof and kicked off of the side. As she soared into the air, the pleasurable rush spread through her brain, and in spite of the direness of the situation, her lips spread into a large grin.

This is bloody fantastic! I almost feel like I can fly. Like I can do anything!

Her pursuers stopped short at the edge of the roof, with the leader of the three holding out his arms protectively against the other two.

"Abort! The Boots are not designed for that far of a jump..."

With mouths agape, the three men watched as their quarry landed safely on the next rooftop almost half a block away, and continue running.

"That shouldn't be possible. She's not wearing Boots and she has no access to CCE."

"A Buff perhaps?" the second man offered.

"There is no Initiator close by performing a Script for her," the first replied.

"It doesn't matter now." The third pursuer chimed in with an authoritative voice. "It's HQ's call." He reached into his jacket pocket and produced a cell phone with which he pressed a button and began speaking.

"Subject has eluded our team by somehow using a Script. Should we continue pursuit?"

A dispassionate voice answered, "Negative. Thanks to your efforts, the subject is entering our location. Return to base."

"Roger that," replied the third man.

Whipping his comm down, he placed it back in his pocket. Staring at their disappearing quarry a moment longer, he turned away walking back to the far edge of the roof, followed by the other two.   Leaping over the side, they disappeared from view.

Laurina continued her flight from the three men, not quite trusting that she had escaped them. Reaching the edge of yet another rooftop she launched herself forward toward another ten-story building.

"Target sighted, "a voice announced from the street.

"In range in five...four..."

"Fire the Sack!" another voice commanded.

"But sir-"

"I said fire!"

A hollow *Boom* echoed at ground level, as a large projectile hurtled skyward.

As the young Brit sailed through the air, the sound of the report caught her attention. She looked down and noticed a small black dot appearing from below. It grew rapidly in size until it appeared to be a large black bundle. All at once, it expanded, and six slim metal arms extended from the perimeter of what was now a large mesh net that was steadily rising up to meet her. As she sailed onward desperately trying to avoid it, her concentration wavered, and she began to panic. All at once a stabbing pain lanced into the redhead's brain causing her to gasp involuntarily, while a feeling of weakness began to spread throughout her entire body.

What happened next was even more frightening. The mysterious flush of power that had initially filled her to bursting had disappeared as if someone had clicked off a light switch. Laurina could sense the last vestiges of warmth leaving her almost as suddenly as it had come, and in its place, a distinct emptiness spread like helplessness throughout her entire being; and she was still ten stories up, in mid-air between the two buildings!

I'm not going to make it.

At that moment, like a metal octopus, the mesh capture sack engulfed her, enclosing the hapless Brit in its fine grey skin while wrapping its dark tentacles around itself in a metal embrace. She felt them tighten quickly, pinning her arms to her side and squeezing her legs together before she could make any defensive move. Struggling was now useless. Laurina Hawks was immobilized with danger fast approaching.

"Got her!" the commander cried out in triumph.

"But Commander Krall," fire control officer replied hesitantly. "She's...she's not going to make the roof sir. Your order was too early."

"What?"

Indeed, the plan was to catch the woman at the apex of her jump, where she would be trussed and cocooned in the Sack before landing safely on the next roof. By firing early, however, the weight of the device came into greater play and began to drag the woman below roof level of the approaching building.

"Dammit! Deploy the bags NOW!" Commander Krall roared.

"Bags deployed sir!"

In reality, it took several milliseconds for the signal to travel from the ground to the Sack's internal microprocessor. Unfortunately, just before the signal was received, the Sack with the woman inside slammed hard against the wall of the building. From inside, came the sickening crunch of bone and a loud cry of pain. The resulting impact sent Laurina reeling into unconsciousness. After a faint beeping noise, a dull thud and a powerful hissing noise became evident as the crash bags began to fill with air. Meanwhile, the Sack with its captive rebounded from the wall and plummeted toward the concrete far below.

The last thing Laurina was aware of was the sensation of falling to her death.

That, and a faint blue glow.

Chapter 4

Waves of exquisite pain washed over Laurina Hawks, bringing her to consciousness with a jolt. A visceral agony throbbed through her as if someone had beaten her entire body with a sledgehammer. She wanted to cry out but her vocal cords were paralyzed, denying her that form of relief. Instead, in her mind's eye, the young Brit gritted her teeth and rode the pain until it finally subsided to a numbing ache. That accomplished, she carefully opened and closed her eyes, wincing from the light until they adjusted to the brightness. There seemed to be a rheumy haze coating her vision but with a bit of effort she could make out the faint outline of the room which she now inhabited. Stark white walls occupied her sight, lined with a variety of lab tables and cabinets. Immediately in front, she saw what looked like a thin blue blanket, and underneath, the outline of legs and feet angled slightly outward toward the left and right.

I'm lying in a hospital bed.

Closer to her prone figure, she could make out the blurry shape of medical equipment and noted grimly that she seemed to be attached to them through an ordered series of cables and tubes. Tracing them back to her arm, she saw that white gauze encased most of her body. Portions of the protective covering were almost completely soaked through with blood which gleamed bright crimson against the harsh light from above. The scent of iron and disinfectant hung heavily in the air.

And I'm in sorry shape to boot!

Feeling something on her head, Laurina lifted her eyes and saw wires tracing down from her forehead to a machine on her right. On the monitor above it danced a myriad of lines not unlike an EEG reading, but these seemed to have no pattern or meaning that she could recognize. She heard a repetitive sound coming from another appliance that undoubtedly monitored her heartbeat. However, at each spike of her heartbeat, the familiar sharp ping of a normal EKG unit was replaced by the echo of an annoying gong, like a mad Asian percussionist trying to gain her attention.

As she tried her best to ignore this latest irritation, Laurina soon became aware of the sound of her labored breathing. Her respiration sounded amplified to her ears as if she were a diver using an aqualung. The overpowering aural timbre rose to assault her hearing while all other sounds receded into the background as if they were muffled through a wall of water. If that weren't enough, the pain in her body that she had so far been able to control, joined the symphony of sensation, throbbing on the downbeat of every breath she took and gaining in intensity. Laurina tried again to focus her mind, but this time the aching washed past her defenses like a breached dam. With each passing moment, her muscles tightened, and the terrible ache became more acute until the pain threatened to totally overwhelm her. She was vaguely aware of a tightness in her throat, and she felt as if the skin on the corners of her lips was about to tear. She also noticed that her vision suddenly jerked left, then right, then left, over and over again.

A vague awareness told Laurina that she was screaming.

Abruptly, a strange chilling sensation in her right arm made itself known, which soon spread throughout her entire body, radiating like a cooling balm. She tried to control her body's movement, but none of her limbs would respond to her mental commands. The jerky back and forth motion of her thrashing about diminished as her tortured muscles released their tightness and relaxed. The coolness seemed to surround the core of her pain and insulate her from it, like an oyster coating an invading piece of grit. The sharp aches were quickly reduced to a shrinking pearl of dull throbbing. Soon it was gone entirely.

Laurina became aware that the few shapes she had come to recognize began to fade from her sight like the ending of a dream. Seconds later, there was nothing left but darkness. The odors that she knew should be there were absent. Neither the pungent antiseptic stench of the hospital room nor the slightly metallic tang of iron emanating from her bloody injuries was detectable. Finally, the incessant beeping from the heart monitor slowly died away from her hearing, echoing into the recesses of her mind. All that remained in the darkness was her breathing, and then the frightening realization that she couldn't even feel the air as it entered her lungs. The beautiful redhead fought panic as her respiration became increasingly more shallow and hurried. Fearful thoughts flooded Laurina Hawk's mind as she lay in the inky void.

Is this the edge of death? Or am I hallucinating again? Dammit, I can't even tell whether I actually lived through the last day or so, or if I dreamed everything that had happened to me since London?

An even more insidious notion wriggled unbidden into her thoughts. Was this some kind of Hell where she was condemned to periods of pain and relief, like a nefariously cruel joke? Or worse, what if she no longer existed at all? What if nothing actually existed outside of herself and everything she once believed had happened was simply the result of her imagination? Memories of the past flowed through Laurina's mind like fuzzy snapshots of time.

"Bugger off!" a chubby 12-year-old Abel yelled, pointing a finger at the boy sitting on a pile of dirty snow holding his now bloody nose. Nearby, Laurina brushed icy slush from a crying Galicia's face. A small bruise began to spread across her left cheek where the lump of coal stashed inside the snowball had hit her.

"I was just 'avin' a bit of fun," the battered boy said. "I didn't hit her that hard."

"Touch my sister again and I'll thrash you so hard that your own mum wouldn't recognize you!" Abel cried.

Seeing that the larger boy meant business, the snowball thrower quickly scrambled to his feet and ran off, trailing dots of blood behind him.

"I'll get you, you fuckin' fatty!" he cried as he ran. "You'll see!"

Ignoring the retreating figure, Abel walked over to his two sisters.

"Are you ok?" he asked Galicia with concern.

After dinner, Laurina and Galicia crept quietly into the dark room on the boy's side of the orphanage searching for Abel. Miss Harbedge had punished him that morning for some vague infraction, but since it was done behind closed doors, no one knew what rule the boy had broken. After giving him a severe beating, the sour woman had sent him up to his room without letting him finish his breakfast, and in addition, he was banned from meals for the rest of the day. She had sternly warned the other children that punishment would be swift and severe for anyone caught bringing him food.

Concerned for their brother, the two girls searched for any sign of the dark-haired boy. They looked around but didn't see him on his bunk. Puzzled, they turned to leave when they heard a liquid growl pierce the silence. Walking towards the source of the sound, they found Abel sitting on the floor between two beds with his back against the wall. The grumble sounded once again into the darkness, and the boy clutched his belly.

"Hell's bells! Was that you?" Laurina whispered.

"Sorry Laur, but I haven't eaten a bloody thing since morning," Abel sighed. "Unless you want to call two mouthfuls of porridge breakfast"

Galicia gazed at him with a look of worry.

"Sounds like you haven't eaten in a week"

Reaching into the pocket of her plaid skirt, she pulled out something about the size of a playing card, wrapped carefully in a paper napkin. Laurina did the same.

"Here Abel," she whispered. "This is for you."

Laurina proffered her own small bundle as well. "And so is this."

The chubby boy unwrapped the napkin and gasped when he saw he was holding a piece of boiled beef. Laurina's bundle revealed a large crescent roll cut open on the side and slathered with mustard. The stunned boy stared first at the perfect sandwich makings then at his two sisters.

"Are you both daft?" Abel exclaimed. "Miss Garbage will kill you if she finds out."

A sly smile appeared on both girls faces.

"We won't tell if you don't," Galicia replied smugly.

Laurina nodded. "Besides, we can't let our protector starve, now can we?"

A thin smile crept onto the chubby face.

"Not bloody manly to have the damsels saving the knight is it?" Abel said while stuffing the piece of beef into the roll.

He paused a bit and looked into the eyes of the two girls.

"Thank you," he whispered. "For being such wonderful sisters."

The dark room grew quiet as the three children regarded each other with thankfulness.

Once again a large growl came from Abel's empty stomach, disturbing the mood.

"Just shut up and eat, you big lout," Laurina smiled blushing.

"...HAPPY BIRTHDAY TO YOU-U-U!" two off-key voices sang.

Laurina jumped up and down excitedly after opening the small white box. Lying inside was the little sterling silver cat pin with rhinestone eyes that she had been coveting for so long.

"Oh, it's marvy! Thank you, Gal! Thank you, Abel! How did you know?"

"Well you kept goin' on about it for the last bloody year," Abel grunted with mock exaggeration.

"It was the only way we could get you to shut up," Galicia chimed in wryly.

"But how did you get the money for it?"

Abel hooked his thumbs into his pockets and puffed out his chest.

"You're lookin' at the new stock boy at Higbee's, love."

"And I had a bit of cash stashed away from working at Molly's Bakery..." Galicia said with a knowing wink.

Tears formed in Laurina's eyes as she wrapped her arms around her sister and big brother, and squeezed them tightly.

"You're the best family any girl could ever have!"

Time seemed to slow as Laurina lay, while memories of the past danced in her head, keeping her company. Each of them was centered around Paddington Foundling Home where she had spent the biggest part of her life. Snatches of various recollections replayed themselves bordered in sepia and gray, like an old rerun of Oliver Twist. Galicia in the school play, Abel at the dance, the three of them fishing just outside of London, or snacking on meat pies at Piccadilly Circus. However, there was something hovering just out of reach of her mind's eye, nagging at the redhead's brain like a sore tooth. Suddenly a bit of realization made itself clear.

I can't remember our parents! I can't remember our home.

I can't remember anything before the orphanage.

It's as if Paddington is the spot where my life first began. And that can't be true, can it?

Can it?

What the hell is happening to me? I feel like I can't even trust my own past anymore.

Surely my memories are proof that I actually had a real life, right?

Right?

A cold shudder past through her and Laurina's thoughts grew cold.

Bloody Hell! I'm losing my mind!

Through this new troubled perspective, her memories now seemed too well ordered, too perfect to be true. Panic gripped the young Brit's heart, and an overwhelming sadness flowed through her mind like tainted water from a shattered dam, threatening to carry her into oblivion.

Laurina felt a tear roll down her cheek. The warm drop of fluid coursed steadily down the skin of her face like a skier descending a hill. Her breathing accelerated with a start, as she realized that she could actually feel the salty flow, and more importantly, that she had caused it to happen. Gathering her courage, the shaken redhead imagined herself floating in an Olympic sized swimming pool.

Gentle movement...my body is bobbing ever so slightly...lightly drifting slightly to the right....while I look up to the skylight! Don't forget the skylight!

Desperately clinging to the image, she stilled her tortured mind and relaxed. After what seemed to be an eternity, Laurina rediscovered her strength of will.

Somehow I am still here, wherever 'here' is, and I am alive. What did Descartes say? "I think, therefore I am!" Well, I'm bloody well thinking alright! Relax old girl and wait it out. Something's gonna happen soon, and when it does, you'll get your answers. Until then you'll just have to be patient.

With a supreme effort, she calmed both her mind and body, accepting the uncertainty of her situation. Her breathing steadied to a more normal pace as she decided that nothing more terrible would happen to her in her current state. There was nothing she could do about it in any case. As Laurina regained her sanity, the shadows slowly receded from her sight. As the view continued to brighten, and the harsh white light chased the last vestiges of the darkness away, two blurred figures that had not been there before, hovered like wraiths on the edge of her awareness.

The two men carefully regarded the broken woman on the exam table. The smaller one clad in a white smock and black horn-rimmed glasses walked to one side, and like a virtuoso played his thin practiced fingers over the banks of buttons and dials on the medical equipment attached to her. He checked the readings and with satisfaction, flipped open a pad to jot down a few notes. Meanwhile, the taller and more imposing of the two stood like a sentinel next to the metal slab, patiently still and ramrod straight, with his arms clasped behind his back as if at attention. His presence radiated *authority and command*; a person used to having his orders followed without question. This was fitting since he was clothed in a crisp blue uniform complete with shoulder patches bearing the Sphinx and dagger motif, which announced his presence as a high-level Army Intelligence officer. His jacket was highly decorated, and including a pair of discs sporting a golden horse head over a chessboard along with the words, "Strength through vigilance." Like a lion guarding his kill, he stood very close and stared intently at his wounded captive.

"When will she be ready Dr. Kelder?" he asked in a gravelly voice.

"I'm not sure," the smaller man replied. "I've stabilized her pain and introduced a compound to accelerate her healing, but these readings indicate a slow recovery. There is no telling how long she could lie in this state."

His superior grunted in acknowledgment while clenching his large hands into fists. "I'll have that idiot Krall's head on a pike for this," he muttered in a low voice.

Kelder waved a thin hand toward one of the medical monitors. "Colonel, come have a look at this." He touched his pen to the EEG monitor as the lines moved excitedly around the screen. "The readings are like nothing I've ever seen before."

"Is there a problem with them?" asked the officer.

"I'm not sure. The subject's readings are erratic. Normal human readouts for someone in her condition would show a slow, steady pulsing of brainwave activity. The impulses here are dancing all over the place."

"Then I suggest you do your level best to get a handle on the situation ASAP," the colonel said tightly. "I shouldn't have to remind you that we are running out of time. If this woman doesn't recover soon, and the Interface closes before we are ready, we will lose our window of opportunity, and everything we have worked for will be lost!"

A dark rumble escaped his lips as the tall man took a menacing step closer to his subordinate. "I sincerely hope that for your sake, doctor, you understand this."

Dr. Kelder took a hasty step backward, covering his fear by appearing to look at the monitor. "Colonel, I am doing the best I can, but we may need a backup plan," he offered. "Perhaps with their technological expertise, the Sempai can find another alternative."

The big man snorted derisively. "Bah! Advanced or not, the Sempai lack the drive and vision required to bring our work to fruition by the appointed time. Even a high school science student has more instinctive creativity and imagination than they will ever have. Your hope in them is badly misplaced Kelder, and that is your weakness." The Colonel lowered his voice to a harsh whisper.   "If you fail to get this woman operational in a timely fashion, I will have you busted down to field medic and have you permanently transferred to a nice little outpost I know in Antarctica. Imagine *that*, doctor."

Confident that he had effectively motivated his assistant, the Colonel turned on his heel and resumed his vigil over the bed holding the young woman. After a brief hesitation, he opened his mouth to speak once again. "On the off chance that you do manage to exceed my expectations, under no circumstances should our little fox be allowed to know that her healing has been accelerated thanks to Sempai technology. I've already instructed Kamla to tell her that she's been in a six-week coma. If the matter comes up, I expect you to do the same."

"Yes Colonel," Kelder replied softly. Chastened, the doctor hung his head and went back to checking the readouts and taking notes. A smile of anticipation played over the commanding officer's lips as he continued to stare at what he hoped to be his greatest accomplishment.

Chapter 5

Laurina's eyes snapped open as if they were spring loaded. Fully alert, she quickly glanced at her arms and legs and found herself to be dressed in purple hospital scrubs. Absent were the wires and tubes that had previously been attached to her body, and there were no signs of scarring or any visible wounds on her flesh. Continuing to take stock of her condition, she noted most importantly that there was no pain. Raising her awareness to take in her surroundings, she saw that the room she now occupied, though windowless, was decorated warmly with robin's egg blue walls, bright but subtle track lighting, and a large framed print of sunlight over a meadow. A vase filled with white lilies and blue irises sat atop a nearby table filling the room with their subtle scent.

The decorations were in stark contrast to the sterile mixture of white and chrome where she first lay, causing her a bit of momentary confusion.

Where am I now? Is this a patient room in a hospital?

The redhead noticed that her body was cradled in total comfort. Behind her head, she could feel the soft cushion of a fluffy pillow and the yielding support of the mattress felt like heaven after the hard slab of the exam table she had first awakened to. A thick blue synthetic blanket had been carefully laid over her body, and the soft fabric caressed her skin like a lover. Moving carefully, she pushed herself up to a sitting position, stopping momentarily as a wave of dizziness came over her. Once it passed, she lifted away the blanket, and slowly swung her legs over the edge of the bed. As the blood rushed through her legs, they felt odd, as if a thousand tiny pins were pricking her skin. Wiggling her pale toes, she grimaced slightly and waited as her slim digits slowly regained their circulation.

A sudden noise to the left snapped her into attention. The knob of the door slowly turned, and in walked a beautiful dark-haired woman of East Indian ancestry clutching a tray filled with an odd assortment of goods. She wore the traditional undersized nurse's cap, and a soft blue smock covered her slim figure. The large white nametag pinned to it announced her as Kamla. The woman smiled brightly as she saw Laurina sitting on the side of the bed, and set her tray down on a stand by the door. She quickly rushed to the redhead's side and with a practiced motion, placed a hand on her forehead.

"I see that our guest is finally awake! How are you feeling love?" Kamla asked musically, scanning her face for anything that looked odd or out of place. As she worked, she caressed the face of her charge in a motherly fashion.

The startled Laurina quickly pulled away from the woman's ministrations.

"Watch the hands, *Love!*" she spoke the last word sarcastically. "Do I know you?"

"Well yes and no," Kamla said cheerily, oblivious to the sarcasm. "I have been caring for you for quite some time now since you had your accident, although you most certainly do not remember it. Oh! Forgive me, you must be parched."

She rose and walked to the sink on the far side of the room. In seconds she was next to redhead again holding a glass of water. Laurina nodded as she took it and drank deeply, frowning in concentration as she did so.

Accident? What...?

Images of leaping off the roof of a tall building tugged at her memory. The recollection of sailing through the air, the uncomfortable feeling of constriction from the mesh sack that had imprisoned her, the looming approach of a brick wall, and the sudden sensation of pain and palpable darkness that swallowed her up slowly rose to the surface of her inner eye.

So, those crazy events had been real after all. London, Brooklyn, the men chasing me, the hospital. Everything had actually happened.

"How long was I out for?" Laurina asked, handing the empty glass back to Kamla.

She smiled back at her before responding.

"Well, you were out for quite a while. Since I came to care for you, I know that you have been out for six weeks. I was beginning to lose hope." Kamla flashed a sympathetic smile.

"Six weeks?!" Laurina exclaimed incredulously.

I must have been comatose to not realize the passage of that much time. Gawd! Abel's gonna kill me! He must be worried sick!

"After six weeks shouldn't my brain be like a vegetable now?"

Kamla placed a palm on Laurina's forehead and became serious. She gently squeezed and probed the contours of her head before removing her hand.

"Hmmm. Well how does your head feel to you?" she asked.

"I don't know," Laurina replied tentatively. "I'm aware and I seem to have control of all of my faculties, so I guess that's all that really matters right?"

"Well, it sure *felt* like a vegetable to me," Kamla replied seriously.

The two women looked at each other for a moment before the nurse erupted in bright laughter. Laurina finally catching the lame joke smiled ruefully and joined in the laughter. Hearing another sound, Laurina followed the nurse's eyes to the doorway. A thin, unassuming man with round glasses and wearing a white lab coat slowly entered the room. A black doctor's bag was nervously clutched in his right hand. Laurina suddenly had the feeling that she recognized him. Nevertheless, she eyed the newcomer with suspicion.

"Doctor Kelder. We've got a live one here!" Kamla chuckled, jerking a thumb toward the seated woman.

Doctor Kelder?

Immediately the redhead's eyes widened in recognition. It was the name from Galicia's letter! *"If they get you trust Kelder..."* Did Galicia mean another Kelder?

This must be the one Gal was talking about, not the bloke from the Yard! If he is, maybe now I can finally get a few answers.

"Are you the one who patched me up?" Laurina asked him nonchalantly.

He nodded to her and smiled, his balding head reflected the light from overhead.

"Kamla," he asked in a gentle voice. "Would you mind giving the lady and I a moment in private?"

"But doctor, I was instructed by Colonel Keren to monitor our patient at all times," the nurse replied uneasily. Laurina's breath caught in her throat as she recognized the name.

"Now Kamla, you know this is a case of patient confidentiality. We're just going to talk doctor to patient. I'll take full responsibility for her condition while you're gone." His eyes narrowed. "Please don't force me into placing an insubordination entry into your file."

Catching the pointed look from her superior, Kamla nodded in recognition.

"Perhaps my help is needed in the supply room anyway. I'll go check on that."

The nurse grasped her patient's hand and smiled at her reassuringly before walking out the door. Laurina, however, was not the least bit reassured.

First Kelder, then Colonel Keren...both names I heard in connection to Gal's predicament. This is crazy! I do one last job, and before I can hook up with Abel and leave for the airport, I'm in Brooklyn New York, and suddenly faced with two people who are possibly involved in this whole flippin' mess. This is NOT a coincidence!

As soon as the door closed behind her, Dr. Kelder rushed to Laurina's side. Before she could open her mouth, he raised a restraining hand.

"Miss Hawks, I'm indeed Dr. Timothy Kelder, and as you've already guessed, it was I who facilitated your healing. I know you have many questions, but we don't have much time. There is much that we need to discuss, and it is very important that you listen to what I have to say." His soft voice coupled with the mention of her sister's name brought sudden recognition.

"So you ARE the Kelder that my sister spoke of!"

"Yes, yes," he replied in a dismissive tone.

Laurina's heart began to pound in her chest like a jackhammer.

"I remember your voice. There were two people hovering over me in my dreams. You were the one defending me, while the other one; well he was just an asshole."

"That asshole was Colonel Keren," Doctor Kelder replied tightly. "But forget that for now. Laurina, will you trust me?" He searched her eyes, and with conviction added, "...for Galicia's sake?"

Laurina paused a moment to think. In her mind's eye, she could see the note and could almost hear the words coming from Galicia's voice, "...Trust Kelder." She sighed heavily.

"Alright, I'll trust you, at least for now. But I need a few answers. First of all, where am I? Where is my sister? Is she alright? What is this place, and how did I even get..."

"Laurina please!" he replied forcefully, waving her to silence.

The anxious redhead startled by his abruptness immediately fell quiet.

Dr. Kelder sighed.

"First things first. You've already gathered that Colonel Keren is not your friend, but it's imperative that he does not suspect that we have spoken like this."

As she nodded her understanding, the doctor listened for any sounds in the hallway. Hearing none, he continued.

"You are in a secret government research facility in an undisclosed location. Your desire to see to the safety of your sister is a part of why you are here right now. To the best of my knowledge, Galicia is still alive, but we have not been in contact with either her or her partner Major Sinza Flanagan for some time. I cannot go into any detail about their mission because the situation is complicated and time-consuming."

"Please tell me what you can," Laurina pleaded.

"There is more going on here than you could ever imagine. The most important thing you need to know is the truth of how you got here and why. You see, you are..."

The sound of approaching footsteps echoed just outside the door.

"Damn it! We're out of time," he whispered.

Laurina whispered back in desperation, "I have what? Tell me! You can't leave me hanging like this!"

"I can't! Not now. I'm truly sorry. Look, for both our sakes, play it close to the vest. Keep your eyes and ears open and I promise you will learn the truth."

The young Brit glared angrily at Kelder.

What's with all this super secret hush-hush stuff? This bloke's treating me like the heroine of a dime store spy novel! He holds out the friggin' carrot and then jerks it away. Screw this 'close to the vest" crap. I need answers now!

Kelder quickly switched into his professional demeanor as a hand fell on the doorknob. Grabbing a shiny stethoscope from his bag, he placed it on Laurina's back as if he's checking her breathing.

"Exhale," he said loudly, just as the door was forcefully opened.

Two military officers strode into the room, both impressively dressed in crisp blue uniforms. Both stopped in unison in front of the redhead and snapped to attention.

"Good day Miss Hawks," the taller of the two greeted her.

In an attempt to cover up her growing irritation, Laurina decided to respond with humor.

"Well, it seems I've been promoted!"

She smiled at her own joke until Kelder shot her a stern glance.

The more decorated cleared his throat, before forcing himself to smile.

"It is nice that you seem to be in the mood for jokes, Miss Hawks. You must be feeling quite fit. I am Colonel Walter Keren."

He gestured to his companion, "this is my subordinate, Corporal Robert Robinson, but you can call him Bob." Bob nodded but remained silent. The Colonel chuckled a bit, trying to sound as warm as possible.

"You're already well acquainted with our Doctor Kelder. The three of us are the coordinators of this little project." Both men regarded the young woman eagerly.

"Project?" Laurina inquired.

"Well you should know," the Colonel replied. "You have already experienced the consequences of what could go wrong. Surely you have come to some conclusion regarding your little...adventure."

Laurina nodded slowly, recognition dawning on her face.

"You 'beamed' me or something," Laurina replied sharply. "First, I was in London, then I was in Brooklyn, and now I am here. I thought pish-posh like this only happened in science fiction movies." The men seemed taken aback by her quick assessment.

"Science fiction?" the Colonel asked in a mocking tone. Then he relaxed and smiled. "Well, I suppose an outsider would think of our process as sci-fi or even magic. Even so, rest assured young lady, we really do 'have the technology.'"

Laurina was quickly losing her patience, in spite of trying to use restraint as Kelder had instructed her to do.

"Listen, mister, I don't give a flying fig how you did it. I just want to know where we are and what I am doing here."

"Our location is classified. As to why you are here…" A smug look appeared on the Colonel's face. "You are here because you fell off the roof of a building and required medical attention."

"Don't patronize me!" Laurina shouted. "Those words seem awfully ironic coming from the ones who trussed me up in that mechanical bag and caused me to miss the mark in the first place."

The colonel's smiling facade slipped just a little.

"That was a regrettable mistake by an overzealous subordinate. Rest assured Miss Hawks, he has been severely punished for causing you harm."

"Oh? Well uh, okay. At least you blokes did a right fine job of mending me up".

"Indeed. And in return for saving your life, we ask only for your cooperation in a small matter." Keren said as he began pacing the room.

"And that would be…"

"An easy job actually. We would just like you to deliver a special disc for us. Nothing more."

Kelder eyed the young woman worriedly, while the man introduced as Bob stood as motionless as a robot. Laurina noticed that something about this request seemed to sit uneasily with the doctor.

"If it is so easy, why don't you deliver it yourself?" Laurina asked.

"Unfortunately we cannot," the Colonel sighed, turning serious. "You must understand Miss Hawks, we've learned rather tragically that not everyone can be teleported.   If you'll come with us, we will explain further."

Colonel Keren started forward, then turned toward the redhead, swept his arm toward the door with a flourish, smiled and waited.

"Fine," Laurina relented. "But if I don't like what you have to say, I'm out." She pushed herself off the bed and immediately fell back against it, as the blood rushed to her limbs, causing an almost painful "pins and needles" sensation in her legs. Kelder began to rush toward her side but froze after getting a piercing look from his superior.

"Perhaps Ms. Hawks would be more comfortable if we were to get her a wheelchair," the doctor offered attentively. "After all, she has been bedridden for quite awhile."

Colonel Keren was about to protest when Laurina waved them away.

"I'm fine, thanks. I just need to get my legs up under me, that's all."

If this pompous colonel wagers that I'm some frilly weakling, he's got another thing coming.   I refuse to give him that satisfaction!

Taking a deep breath and pushing herself to her feet, Laurina moved her steadying hands off the bed. She attempted several deep knee bends, while the three men waited patiently, each one becoming easier to do. The spasms finally subsided, and she took a few tentative steps. Her knees were still a bit shaky, but with a little concentration, the young Brit found she was able to walk with more confidence.

"Alright, let's be off then," she nodded to the Colonel.

"Very well. Please, follow us." Keren said, exiting the room.

Dr. Kelder fell in step behind the tall Colonel and Laurina trailed behind him. Corporal Robinson closed the door and brought up the rear.

The long corridor was dimly lit with blinking fluorescent lights. Cables and cording ran like oversized snakes along the ceiling, while heavy piping and air ducts jutted out from the grey walls with no apparent rhyme or reason.   It was a marked contrast to the cheery blue patient room.   Laurina also noted the absence of people in the halls. No other doctors, nurses, patients or even visitors roamed the somber corridor. The silence was eerie.

This is the strangest damn hospital I've ever seen.

The concrete floor that they walked on felt cold to Laurina's bare feet, and she instantly missed the warmth of her bed. Walking gingerly across the icy feeling surface, she grumbled to herself.

They could have at least given me a crummy pair of paper booties to wear.

Nevertheless, not wanting to appear weak in front of these men, she kept her complaints to herself and continued walking. The group finally turned down a corner, and a single door stood at the end of a short hallway. Keren stopped in front of it and entered a code sequence into an electronic keypad. After several beeps, there was a smooth mechanical sound, and suddenly four banks of .50 caliber guns emerged from the walls on both sides, and with a whine of servos, pointed their barrels directly at the group.

"Bugger me!" Laurina exclaimed while jumping backward.

An angry robotic voice challenged the party from unseen speakers.

"You have initiated the Voice Recognition sequence. You have one attempt. State your name and code phrase or face termination! You have ten seconds".

A digital number "10" in red appeared above the keypad and began its countdown.

9

8

7...

Laurina shot a glance at Colonel Keren, who stood smiling at the door but saying nothing. Afraid to speak in fear of disrupting the process, she grabbed a hold of Doctor Kelder's arm, peering anxiously into his eyes.

6

5...

The small man sighed. He had seen this game before.

Kelder discretely cleared his throat.

"This is Colonel Walter Keren...Hammerfall," his superior declared smugly.

Immediately the weapons retracted into their niches, and the keypad flashed a deep green.

"Please enter Colonel Keren," the voice invited in a more humble tone.

A sharp metal sound of bolts disengaging split the air, and the door slowly yawned open of its own accord. Keren strode quickly inside as if he were a father arriving home to his family, followed at a slower pace by the others. Grey shadows seemed to envelop them, and the murky darkness masked what lay inside

As Laurina's eyes adjusted, she saw that the room was filled with an array of various technologies, some of which she had never seen before, packed along every inch of the walls. While the space itself was large, the room seemed unduly cramped and claustrophobic. Multi-colored lights and indicators played along their surfaces as the machinery was busy processing information and making calculations. In the center of the room sat an oversized padded armchair with a control console facing it. Dual monitors flared to life as Keren walked over to the workspace and tapped the keyboard twice. A low hum could be heard escaping from the devices, giving a signal that all was in readiness. Satisfied, he turned back to address their 'guest'.

"Teleportation, as I mentioned earlier, is not something just any person can do. After much testing and experimentation, we have discovered that in order to transport a human being from one location to another, it all comes down to the person's basic genetic structure and its code within the genome. I won't bore you with the technical aspects of our discovery, other than to say that those who are candidates contain a certain "X-factor." It is a rare gift, and only a very small few possess this capability. You, young lady, are one of those few.

"Tell me, Miss Hawks, do you have any understanding of quantum physics?" Keren asked, walking slowly over to her and the rest of the group.

"Not one bit," she said.

Mildly disappointed, Keren sighed.

"Well, unfortunately, we have neither the time nor the resources with which to properly educate you." The Colonel turned and paced back to the desk. "So you are just going to have to take this on faith."

A predatory smile emerged from his lips at the last two words. His smile disturbed Laurina. She knew immediately that it wasn't an expression of his good humor, but rather derived itself from some sadistic pleasure that only he could see.

"Well my lack of knowledge aside, you have already teleported me once. There is no reason to think that you can't do so again." Laurina replied guardedly.

"Good. Then we'll begin with the briefing." The tall man nodded once and Corporal Robinson, who had been silent the whole time, immediately stepped forward and began to speak. This surprised Laurina, who was beginning to think that Keren's subordinate was little more than window dressing.

"Miss Hawks," he intoned in an oddly flat voice. "You will be sent to the last known location of two of our operatives, in a classified city in New Mexico. Once established, you will seek out a Major Sinza Flanagan..."

He passed a translucent tablet to Laurina which held a picture of an athletic looking black-haired woman on the monitor. Robinson tapped the device in her hands, and the image changed to that of a familiar face.

"...and her aide Galicia Hawks. Both are part of this institution and have disappeared during a recent mission. It seems they found themselves in an unpleasant situation and had to go into hiding."

Laurina's blood grew cold as she looked intently at the picture of her own sister.

Ahhh, there's the kicker. This confirms that the message was from Gal after all. And she is in some kind of trouble.

"And just what do you mean by 'an unpleasant situation'?" Laurina asked warily. She reminded herself silently to heed Doctor Kelder's warning and play the situation coolly, rather than give these military men the satisfaction of knowing how distressed she was about her sister's welfare. She placed her hands on her hips and waited for a response, all the while feeling like she was about to burst. Corporal Robinson glanced at the Colonel for permission to answer. Keren nodded for him to continue.

"The teleportation system that we use is housed at the classified location within an energy shield. There is a gateway there as well. Both operatives failed to return through it during the allotted mission period, and due to a lack of genetically suited personnel, no one else has attempted to go through to meet them. It is imperative to the project, and for the safety of our operatives that we get certain information to them ASAP."

Keren's subordinate produced something small and dark from his pocket and held it at eye level.

"The classified information is encoded within this disk. It also contains a special sensor that will temporarily disable the energy field and enable you to enter the facility. Your mission will be to search for the missing operatives. When you make contact with them, give them the disk. Once they decode their instructions, they will quickly carry out their orders, and then return home with you."

Robinson allowed Laurina to examine the object- a non-descript plastic rectangle that resembled a flash drive, but with one difference. This 'disk' contained two shiny prongs on one end.

"Sure doesn't look like any disk I've ever seen before," she commented dryly.

After allowing her to examine it a few seconds, he deftly plucked the object from her hands and placed it back in his jacket.

Laurina paused a moment to soak everything in.

There's more to this than they are telling. That is certain.

Colonel Keren turned to the redhead expectantly. His expression was all business.

"Will you cooperate with us Miss Hawks?" he asked.

She understood immediately that his request was really a demand.

"Do I have a choice?" she replied.

Keren chuckled grimly.

"Honestly, no. If you were to decline, we couldn't let you leave this facility with the knowledge of this operation and the teleportation device. You'd probably find yourself with selective amnesia and struggling to choose a new bed at Scotland Yard to suit your taste. We would also be forced to connect you and your orphanage to the stolen money. Of course, the Yard would probably have to shut it down."

"You bastard!" Laurina spat through clenched teeth.

"There is also the fate of the two operatives to be considered. After all, who knows what may happen to Major Flanagan and...your sister?" Keren let the comment dangle in the air while the redhead seethed. Motioning to his subordinate, he waited as the man pulled an item out of the drawer of a nearby cabinet and handed it to him. It was her briefcase!

"But if you cooperate, the 250,000 pounds that you uh, acquired will be given back to you, with interest of course, and the authorities can remain in the dark about it and any of your other associations."

Snapping open the case, the officer displayed the contents to the young woman, to allay any doubts. No mistake. It was the money she purloined from Rickenbacher. In one fluid motion, he snapped the case closed and tossed it back to Robertson, who promptly returned it to the cabinet. Once again, Keren's predatory smile reappeared.

Laurina gave the colonel a look that would have melted iron.

"Before I do anything, I need to make a call to London..." she began.

The Colonel held up a hand to cut her off.

"I'm sorry, but I'm afraid that your brother or anyone else will have to remain in the dark for a little while, due to the sensitive nature of this situation. However, once this assignment is completed, I will make it up to your entire family by providing you all with a 30-day vacation to the destination of your choice, first class, all expenses paid; compliments of the United States government."

Once again he presented the redhead with a large smile.

"Can you ask for a better family reunion?"

It's like being face to face with a Bull shark who promises not to eat you. I don't trust this bloke any further than I can throw him. I'd love to tell him to piss off, but there is Galicia to consider. If I say no, we are both screwed. And if I say yes...
The blighter's got me by the short hairs!

"Very well." she relented. "I'll deliver your bloody disk."

"Outstanding!" Keren beamed. "Bob?"

The Colonel's assistant produced a brown bundle and handed it to the reluctant woman.

"Here, put this on," he intoned stiffly.

Touching a stud in the wall, a bank of machinery slid outward and to the left, revealing a hidden inner chamber. It was well lit, illuminated be some type of recessed lighting. With just a hint of hesitation, Laurina walked into it alone. Once she crossed the threshold, the bank of machinery slid shut behind her.

The space resembled a very utilitarian locker room, without the lockers. The walls were made almost entirely of gray cinder block and cement, and its only furnishings were a tall department store mirror on one wall, and a metal bench bolted to the floor on the other end. Looking behind, she saw a stud on the wall similar to the one the corporal used. Nearby was a small circular dot. Her training told her exactly what it was...A surveillance camera.

"Lovely," Laurina muttered.

After only a moment's hesitation, she set the brown bundle down and slipped out of the clothes Kamla had dressed her in, laying them carefully on the bench beside her. Conscious of the camera and her nakedness, she quickly unwrapped the strange brown bundle which turned out to be some sort of military incursion outfit. It was a stretchy one-piece garment that was worn like a union suit. Sitting on the bench Laurina pulled the material over one leg and raised an eyebrow. The dark fabric felt like leather to the touch but was cool and breathable. After getting her second leg in, she reached behind and grabbed the upper portion and squeezed into it. The military suit zipped up from the waist to just under her chin and fit her snugly, hugging the curves of her body like a second skin. Several black zippered pockets were conveniently placed at the waist and hips, along with a number of loops which seemed to be designed for a utility belt of some kind. There were no shoes included with the outfit, but she noticed that it did have padded soles. It certainly felt like she was wearing shoes but without the bulk and weight to her feet. She jumped up and down a few times and stretched from side to side to test its flexibility. The suit was not only light but gave the impression of being very durable.

She turned to where she had entered, touched the stud and the wall opened once more. Laurina emerged from the small room and approached the waiting Colonel.

"Is all this really necessary?" she asked, gesturing to her outfit.

"Yes, it is, unfortunately," Keren shrugged. "You are going into rough terrain and this suit will protect your body from minor scratches and abrasions. Besides, they are standard issue to all of our operatives." As he spoke, Robinson walked over to his side and handed him the disk.

"Keep this on your person at all times Miss Hawks, and please do not lose it," he said, placing the small plastic device into her hand. "Not only will it temporarily deactivate the energy shield, but the information it contains is of the utmost importance. It must reach Major Flanagan and Ms. Hawks."

Keren gestured towards the oversized padded chair in the center of the room.

"Come sit."

Laurina placed the disk into a hip pocket and zipped it closed. Satisfied, she walked over and eyed the recliner suspiciously. There were both body and arm restraints protruding from it that she hadn't noticed earlier. Nearby Dr. Kelder stood at a console with a look of anxiety on his face. Reluctantly she sat and tried to prepare herself for what was to come.

Alright, old girl. No sense crying about it now. Relax and get it over with, and we'll see you on the other side.

Willing her body into a state of calm, Laurina allowed Kelder to secure her to the chair.

"Good luck, and be careful," he whispered as he made a final adjustment. Soon the doctor moved back to the console and flipped on several switches. Immediately she felt an electric field surrounding her body. The intensity increased steadily, making her skin feel like there were ants crawling over her. Satisfied that all was ready, Dr. Kelder nodded to the Colonel.

"I neglected to tell you Miss Hawks" Keren suddenly announced. "There will be some ...disorientation, but that will pass. Just remember your mission, to deliver the disk without fail!"

His silent assistant hovered next to Dr. Kelder at the main panel and pulled down on a lever. Laurina reflexively closed her eyes, and a strange tingling feeling made its presence known within her body. Soon the intensity of the electric sensation began to increase exponentially, making her feel as if the ants were beginning to bore into her skin. There was no pain, but a noticeable pressure squeezed against her from all sides. A moment later the room seemed to pitch, and the young Brit felt as if her body were being ripped apart. Not limb from limb, but on a molecular level. Suddenly there was a sickening lurch and, even with her eyes closed, Laurina could sense that her surroundings were beginning to change.

Chapter 6

"So, exactly what the hell are we doing out here Sarge?" asked Specialist Nathaniel Hull as they pedaled closer and closer to their destination.

Sergeant Cyrus Briggs stared straight ahead as he maneuvered their craft toward the shadowy landscape of the Shrouded Isle, so named due to the thick fog that blanketed the landmass, making observation impossible.

"We are supposed to take readings around the island, Nathaniel," he said matter-of-factly.

"Why do you think we're carrying all of these electronics in this tub, Null," Specialist Walter Boyd chided, indicating the packs in the center of the makeshift craft with a large meaty arm as he pedaled. "Damn. Don't you pay attention at all to the briefings?"

Hull gave his companion a dirty look.

"Screw off, Wall. If I want to know something about creampuffs and triple-decker sandwiches, I'll ask you."

"And If I want to ask a question of someone with a brain, I won't ask you." came the reply.

Briggs had had enough.

"Button it, both of you, 'fore I throw both your sorry asses overboard!"

The two men fell into a brooding silence- each one eyeing the other but staying quiet.

The sergeant shook his head ruefully. From the time the three of them had arrived at Diamond Head and put the advanced pedal-powered craft into the water until now, his subordinates had been running their mouths. It was bad enough to pull this boring assignment in the first place. But to have these two assigned to him? Sure, they were both capable soldiers-above average in fact. And it was well known that in reality, they were the best of friends, but you wouldn't think so by the way they berated each other at every turn. Someone higher up must've thought it was a perverse joke to assign these two to work together. While technically the Specialists performed their assignments in exemplary fashion, they constantly bickered with each other like an old married couple. And this time, the Aeternus Brass had made him the marriage counselor.

He hated it.

Nathaniel Hull was the Research Operations Specialist (ResOp). He was tall, spare and gangly, and his wheat-colored hair gave him the appearance of one of the scarecrows on Briggs' great-grandfather's farm. His bland, questioning look, made him seem less than intelligent, which was why Walter corrupted his last name into "Null." However, Nathaniel was extremely inquisitive, and he would constantly ask questions, trying to find out every detail and every nuance he could about a given subject or problem. His inquisitive nature made him perfectly suited for Research Operations. In spite of his appearance, he was near genius level, possessing an eidetic memory for facts and all manner of information, and could recall things at will. He had recently received an invitation to join a think tank sponsored by the Sempai led Institute of Creative Culture after his tour of duty with the Aeternus Military was completed. Anyone who underestimated Nathaniel's intelligence due to his looks did so at their own peril.

Walter Boyd was the Technical Operations Specialist (TechOp). He was a 300-pound lump of a man who labored under the belief of his own mental and physical superiority. An expert in both high tech gadgetry and hand to hand combat; he was loud, brash and a bit of a blowhard, but his skills made him well able to back up his bravado. Like Hull, he was highly intelligent, and near genius level. He could fix practically anything and had been tapped on several occasions to design vehicles for the Aeternus military. He was also a great guy to have in a fight, except for the fact that he would bore you to tears about his part in it afterward. Because of his girth, Nathaniel always referred to him as "Wall," to Walter's eternal irritation.

Privately, Master Sergeant Cyrus Briggs of Aeternus Intelligence (IntOp) couldn't help but think of these two jokers by the nickname given to them by the Aeternus rank and file soldiers, "Null and Void."

A handsome, coffee-skinned man with boyish charm, Briggs had worked hard in the Aeternus army to shed himself of his "pretty boy" image. He had honed himself both physically and mentally, to be the best soldier he could be, and was determined to make his family proud. During boot camp, he outworked every one of his peers, gaining in strength and agility, while sculpting his 6-foot frame to become the "Lean, mean, fightin' machine" that his superiors so desperately desired in their men. He was an expert marksman and an even more formidable fighter than Boyd. However, his prowess was not limited to just the physical.

A "non-linear thinker" with a keen analytical ability, Briggs had a knack of solving problems in nonconventional ways, which gained him the respect of his peers who referred to him as "the answer man." Even his immediate superiors consulted him on occasion for particularly thorny problems. Kindly and humble, he was always there for his peers, and later, for the men he commanded. But no one mistook his caring demeanor for weakness. Anyone who attempted to intimidate, or out think him, quickly found themselves outwitted, outgunned and overmatched. After the encounter, some would quietly choose a different duty station, while others left the military entirely, unwilling to chance any more humiliation from this quiet man.

Eventually, his abilities got him noticed by the Brass. Executive Officer Nehemiah Kuma himself, a hard man to impress at the best of times, recognized his officer potential immediately and took a liking to him. He carefully guided the young man's career path over the last few years, placing him in situations that he thought would foster his leadership abilities, and bring out the best in him.

"I know it will be a challenge Cyrus," Kuma would say. "But I have faith that you'll shine. Besides, adversity builds character."

...Which brought him to this Op, and his two bickering subordinates.

Glancing at them, he sighed. They weren't bad guys. They were just irritating at times. He cleared his throat twice before addressing them.

"To answer your question Nate, I'll reiterate our mission. Keep in mind that this is restricted Intel okay? The Seer in Preguntas contacted the Brass about a small but strange reduction of power emanations from Shrouded Isle. Our job is to measure and get confirmation of this. We were each chosen for this mission due to our particular talents, and we're gonna put them all to good use. Now, are we clear on this mission?"

"Yes, Sir!" answered Specialist Hull.

"Roger that," affirmed Specialist Boyd.

"Good," replied Briggs. "We'll be arriving soon, so let's get that gear unpacked and ready for use!"

"Yes, Sir!" both men answered.

Chapter 7

Due to the extremely high salinity and acidic characteristics of the Canis Strait, other than several species of worms and cephalopods, there was not much sea life that existed there. The greenish-black open waters of Nedara were known to be toxic to human life. In fact, after five minutes of exposure, human skin begins to break down rapidly, and without chemical intervention, the victim would hemorrhage to death. This necessitated the use of special protective suits to be worn when traveling on the strait. The water was also very hard on any material that rested upon it or over it for longer than 30 minutes, breaking down its molecular structure, and in the case of a watercraft, eventually rendering it non-seaworthy. This made water travel extremely hazardous.

To complicate matters even further, Core Conversion Energy was practically useless in this zone. Even the air above the water's surface was such that any machine or piece of equipment running on CCE would be drained of power in a relatively short period of time. This made large vehicles unpractical and any smaller watercraft that dared to venture out into the deep had to be specially shielded, and be operated manually. The three Aeternus soldiers were in such a craft.

Along with the traditional metals and polymer plastics that most boats were built with, this one was lined with multiple layers of Endura, a material similar to Kevlar in nature, and finally covered in a seven-layer skin of Elastec. If left in this environment, however, even this bolstered craft, as tough as it was, would in time eventually degrade into un-usability. The lightweight 6-meter vessel was essentially a high tech paddleboat, where several members could sit in a special compartment, and while adopting a cyclist's posture, they would operate pedals which would propel the boat through the water. The pedals were attached to a series of midsized paddles which were specially designed to channel and multiply each pedal revolution to create the most efficient use of the force applied. The resulting compounded effort could propel the craft to speeds of 10-12 knots under heavy exertion from one man alone. Doubly fast with two.

Specialist Boyd was especially proud of the vessel since he had a major part in its design. In fact, he was actually co-owner of the patent on Elastec. As they moved out, he called out to the Master Sergeant at the helm.

"How's it handling Sarge?"

Briggs smiled. "Like a dream Walter. Like a dream!"

Nathaniel smiled ruefully. "C'mon Sarge, don't say that. You're just going to make him even more insufferable than he already is."

"Can you say jealousy?" Boyd quipped. "I knew you could."

The conversation between the men soon sobered as they approached their mist-covered objective. Once the thick fog began to envelop their position, Briggs ordered them to reduce their speed. As the gurgling propulsion of the high tech craft slowed, and an eerie calm settled over the waters, words ceased entirely. Maneuvering carefully, the three men finally arrived at the coordinates of the five-mile barrier around the Shrouded Isle.

Since time began, the island home of the mysterious figure known as the Guardian of the Source, and the WellSpring, the source of all power within Nedara, had been surrounded by a force field to keep humans out, while birds and other wildlife could come and go as they pleased.

Over the millennia, many had tried to break this field. Most tried to attack it through the air without success. Several foolhardy men tried to make a surface approach using a combination of reinforced thick hulled skiffs and augmented swimmers suits. Unfortunately, not only did they fail to penetrate the island's barrier, but the corrosive waters proved too much for their equipment, and as their skiff sank, the entire party suffered a grisly death. A few enterprising individuals had even designed a makeshift probe that was lowered into the toxic waters, along the edge of the field to see if it indeed ran down to the seafloor. However, each attempt met with failure as the camera picture would inevitably "wink out "after 10 minutes of lowering, with the force field present on the camera until the end. Eventually, no one even bothered trying anymore. It had become an accepted fact in the consciousness of all Nedarans, that no one could gain entrance to this mysterious place. In fact, in the language of Nedara, the euphemism "trying to breach the field" became synonymous with attempting the impossible.

As hard as the three men tried, the island could barely be seen due to the dense fog bank that surrounded it at all times. Although it was a sunny day, the natural light was diffused by the surrounding mist, giving Briggs' dark brown skin a grayish cast, and his two subordinates, the ashen color of the living dead. What little of the hilly shoreline that could be seen in the distance, looked to the soldiers like a gateway to the underworld.

The scientific equipment they carried, while powered by CCE, was heavily shielded as well, allowing them about an hour of use before all power was drained

"Commencing readings Sarge," Nathaniel called out.

"Roger that."

"Checking power emanations Sir," Walt murmured, studiously observing his portable scanner. Briggs smiled. It was the most serious his two subordinates have been all day.

"Alright, gentlemen. The barrier would normally be about t ahead at this point," he announced. "I am going to guide us forward slowly, using your readings as a guide. I don't have to say that I am counting on your accuracy."

"Yes sir!" the two men barked, as they pored over their scanners.

Briggs tucked himself inside one of the two propulsion modules, and gently pushed the pedal by foot.

"Easing ahead at minimal."

Several moments went by as the special craft slowly inched forward. But they met with no resistance whatsoever.

"Sarge, I've got no visual confirmation," Hull said. "Usually at this range, we should be able to see the water lap up against it, but I've got zero. No water displacement, no splashing, nothing."

Boyd nodded as he spoke.

"He's right, Sarge. Short range scanners aren't picking up anything either and we are...about ninety meters inside the normal perimeter!"

Sergeant Major Briggs grunted in surprise. "Indeed? Well, perhaps these strange waters are affecting our position. Continuing to proceed."

Slowly he propelled them forward meter by meter, but still, there was nothing to impede their progress. Twenty minutes later, he called out for more readings.

"I'm getting faint readings Sarge, but they are..." Nathaniel gasped. "This can't be right. Damn, my unit must be busted."

"What is it, Specialist?"

"I see it too Nate," Boyd called out soberly.

"Okay gentlemen...d'ya mind letting me in on this intel?"

"Er, right Sarge. Sorry," the lean soldier apologized.

Walter shook his head. "It's just that, it's incredible Sarge. The Seer was right. The field is 4.8 kilometers ahead of us."

"In other words, we've already come three kilometers within the shield's normal placement."

"Yessir," the larger man affirmed. "But that's not all..."

Nathaniel chimed in with amazement in his voice. "The field is shrinking as we speak Sarge. We'll need to get right up on it for me to measure the rate of decrease, but it is definitely shrinking in size."

"What's even more disturbing is...well... sir," Boyd chimed in again before pausing in indecision.

"What is it, Walter?"

"Well Sarge, I can't factually say for sure yet, but preliminary findings are showing that not only has the size of the island's field decreased, but the power emanations from the island itself are dwindling as well. Both are continuing to decline at a steady rate."

This was unheard of. It took Sergeant Major Briggs several seconds of silence to absorb the information, not to mention what their findings suggested. The implications were staggering.

"Alright, gentlemen. I agree that these preliminary findings are incredible, to say the least. However, I'd feel a lot better if we had some hard evidence to go along with these readings. I don't know how much time we have left before the equipment starts to degrade, so let's make the most of it. We're going right up to the barrier itself. Moving ahead at half speed."

Briggs pumped the pedals faster, and the craft jumped into motion. The men could hear the cool salty breeze rush past the ear holes of their protective suits as the Sergeant Major exerted himself. The quiet aboard the craft was palpable, as the normally talkative Specialists were silent; choosing instead to monitor their equipment, while pondering the meaning of this new revelation. Soon, Specialist Hull called out.

"Now reading the barrier at one-hundred meters away Sarge."

"Very good," the Sergeant replied. "Slowing to minimal. We'll let her momentum ease us in close."

"Readings are strong, sir." Specialist Boyd said.

"Gentlemen, it's show time," Briggs announced.

The watercraft drifted slowly ahead through the misty water, as the two Specialists scanned for the barrier and took energy readings. Sergeant Briggs waited patiently, pondering the situation as he waited for their report. Soon a faint but pleasant humming could be detected emanating ahead of their position, which grew louder as the men approached the Shrouded Isle.

The gentle sound rose and fell rhythmically as if it were the heartbeat of the island itself. Finally, the mist they were traveling through lifted a bit, and they could finally see the land mass directly ahead of them. A moment later, a soft jolt hit the craft at it made contact with the island's impenetrable force field. It resembled a large plate glass window which rose high and straight into the air from where they had come to rest. At a distance, if the mists shifted just right, you could tell that it curved away toward the island's interior. It had a slight bluish cast like the cellophane used to decorate popcorn balls.

Briggs reached out with a hand and ran it across the smooth obstruction that only a few had ever touched. It displayed an oddly comforting warmth upon contact and vibrated lightly and rhythmically like a glass table would in a room filled with operating machinery. The two Specialists took this rare opportunity and touched the thrumming transparent barrier themselves, gasping in wonder at the contact. After a while, the duo murmured to themselves in technical jargon, checking and confirming the information they had garnered until finally reaching a consensus.

"Alright men," their commander spoke soberly. "Let's have it."

Hull and Boyd looked at each other knowingly, before the thinner of the two spoke first.

"Sarge, the Seer was definitely right. The field is shrinking at a rate of approximately 16.8 meters per hour. That means that it will make landfall in about 96 hours."

"Four days," Briggs spoke aloud. "What about the power emanations?"

Boyd spoke up this time. "Well, I have confirmed that the amount of Proto CCE being produced from the island is diminishing at roughly the same rate. Something strange is definitely going on over there."

"Speculation? Any ideas as to the cause of this power drain?"

Again, the two specialists murmured together for a moment, before turning back to the Sergeant Major.

"We can only come up with two reasons for this phenomenon," Nathaniel began. "One, the Guardian is drawing power to himself to conserve energy, for some unknown purpose, or..."

"Or," Walter continued. "What we see here is the result of the diminishing of residual energy."

Cyrus Briggs immediately knew where this was headed, and spoke aloud the words that they were all thinking.

"...Meaning that the Guardian is no longer there. He is gone."

The two Specialists looked at each other and nodded.

"Affirmative Sarge. As crazy as it sounds, the Guardian may have left the Shrouded Isle," finished Walter.

"If that were true," Nathaniel asked. "What would it mean Sarge? I mean, for all of us, and for life in our world?"

Briggs fell silent, once again pondering the fantastic implications of this revelation. Finally, he sighed heavily before addressing his men.

"Gentlemen, honestly I can't say at this point. Keep in mind, even with the evidence we've gathered here, we really don't *know* anything yet. This is still supposition on our part at this point. It's pretty clear that there's more to this mystery than we've been told, and that info is above our pay grade. We need to get this Intel to the Brass ASAP without attracting the attention of the Draconians."

Boyd spoke up. "Well, that means we can't radio over water. The Dracs will pick it up for sure."

The Aeternus mission commander nodded soberly before drawing himself up to his full height. When he spoke again, his subordinates could hear the steel in his voice and knew he meant business.

"Assume your stations, men. We're going to sprint back to the mainland as fast as our legs can carry us, get this intel to the Towers, and let them figure out a course of action."

Briggs maneuvered the craft away from the barrier, pointing the bow back the way they came. His mouth set in a grim line. "Let's see how fast this baby can go."

Chapter 8

Laurina Hawks stood alone and disoriented in an empty hallway. She was slightly bent forward as she cradled her head in her hands, fighting to regain her equilibrium. Slowly the gray corridor came into focus. The spangling lights that attacked her eyes had faded, but she still felt a slight buzzing in her ears. A sensation of cool air enveloped her body, and as she looked down she saw her own nakedness. An instant later she was back to being fully clothed.

What the hell? Did I just imagine losing my clothes? I must be more out of it than I realized.

She had no idea what happened to her body after being teleported by Keren's machine, but she knew she wasn't anxious to repeat it.

Bloody hell! It felt like being dragged through a fucking keyhole!

Mercifully, the aural assault faded, and the young Brit was finally able to stand erect and take in her surroundings. The hall opened up at one end, to a large warehouse of some sort, while at the other end, it seemed to continue a good ways toward a series of offices. However, she also saw strange obstructions throughout the corridor, as if the very walls had sprouted and placed parts of itself throughout the opening. At one point a small area of the corridor was riddled with needle-like darts embedded into the walls on both sides like a pin cushion. Moving carefully, Laurina noticed that a twenty-meter section of the floor was missing just ahead of her. Walking to the edge, she leaned over and saw that the smooth sides of this large opening descended to an equally smooth floor thirty meters down.

What the hell is this? An uncovered trap? And why are sections of the wall projecting toward the center of the corridor? It couldn't have been built that way!

Once again she was getting that Alice in Wonderland feeling. Left with no other choice, Laurina headed toward the open area. A thick layer of dust coated the floor, leaving puffs of small gray clouds at every step. She noticed that as she walked, she was leaving very conspicuous looking footprints behind.

She emerged from the hallway into the larger room, looking from side to side with surprise. Large chunks of concrete, shattered wooden crates, and other debris littered the floor, partially hiding what looked to be scorch marks from some sort of blast. Spatters of a viscous brown pigment were dribbled in haphazard patterns on the gritty floor, and as the young woman got closer, her nostrils wrinkled at a strong unmistakable odor.

Blood! Gods, it looks like World War three broke out in here.

Following the blast patterns with her eyes, she could see that some of the ashy smears covered several places along one wall, and seemed to be concentrated toward a grated stairwell on her right and the open office area upstairs. There were more stains of blood in this area, including several small pools of it in a circular pattern near the battered set of metal stairs. With curiosity getting the better of her, Laurina ascended them to the top of the metal catwalk, careful to step over several holes where the metal had been blasted through by some sort of weapon. Keeping a hand on the rail, she turned right toward the office and marveled at the destruction in front of her. The wall that fronted the room, along with most of the door-jam was almost completely destroyed. Shattered glass, plaster and twisted metal were all that remained. Further inside, she saw evidence that a fire had taken place. It must have been quite hot since there was a lot of blackened plastic melted into a semblance of gobs of greasy wax; the remains of a mainframe computer console, monitors and a number of other larger pieces of equipment. There was no indication of power running through any of them, and the darkened hardware gave the appearance of being unused for a long time. A crusted tinge of blue fire retardant covered everything in the room. Smaller chunks of concrete were scattered about, and a thick layer of plaster dust coated the shattered office as well. Curiously there was no blood on the floor here.

Bloody glad I wasn't here when this happened!

Moving back down the stairs, Laurina couldn't help but think that the ones being shot at may have been her sister and Major Flanagan.

The warehouse brightened and she noticed that a shaft of sunlight was shining brightly through a large hole in the center of the ceiling, and through another on the wall on the right. She put a hand to her face to block out the light, as she looked up to examine both openings. The hole in the roof was perfectly circular, and it gave the appearance of being carved from the bottom up. Just what made the cut was anyone's guess. The hole in the wall, however, told its own story. It was obvious that someone had blown it open with explosives. Burned and shattered rubble lay scattered on the floor around it, and the wall was scorched black around its jagged edges like the dead remains of a giant campfire. The air was still, and dust motes floated lazily in the shafts of sunlight like miniature fireflies.

Laurina walked over and lightly kicked at the debris. A few pieces of concrete cascaded down and dislodged a large metal pipe which crashed to the floor, kicking up a cloud of dust at its collapse. She had deftly leaped out of the way at its fall, but could not avoid the quickly moving particles now in the air. Set to coughing by the dust cloud, she moved toward the opening, seeking the clearer outdoor air. After a few tentative steps, she was through the breach in the wall, and away from the spreading haze. Taking refuge along the outer wall several meters away, she coughed hard, clearing her irritated lungs. After the redhead recovered her breath, she turned her attention to her surroundings.

The redhead saw that she was standing near a gravel path that wound its way up from the entrance of the warehouse. Outside the gate lay a dusty road that was sparsely lined on one side by a few ancient storefronts, and what appeared to be an abandoned filling station. It continued on toward a very small and weather-worn western town. A perfusion of sagebrush and cacti marked the fields along the way, adding a bit of color to the drab landscape. Several grayish houses could be seen about a quarter mile away, but they looked lonely and forgotten.

Curious, the redhead slowly walked toward the storefronts, stepping over piles of rusted gears and bolts lying atop the gravel. Carefully slipping through the dilapidated chain link fence that marked the warehouse complex property line, she made her way to the dirt road, stopping in front of an old abandoned diner. A warm desert breeze rattled the rusted screen door against the frame of the deserted eatery's entrance, while a large tumbleweed freed itself from the hood of a broken down car parked in front, and rolled back toward the warehouse.

This looks like a scene from the Twilight Zone.

A rusty barbed wire fence ran behind the diner marking the boundaries of the property, while a metal sign hanging above the entrance that read "Mother's Luncheonette" creaked eerily in the wind. Down the road to the south, a rusty white water tower stood like a silent sentinel guarding a scattering of rusted fifty-gallon drums stacked nearby. Its weathered face which had once proudly heralded the name of the town had long since been scoured clean by wind, sand and time. Small drops of water trickled from the tower and collected into a large puddle below.

She could see for kilometers in both directions, and not a single moving vehicle could be spotted. To the north, she had a better view of the ancient gas station which was surrounded by several old cars that had clearly seen better days. Beyond the gas station lay a few stunted trees straining for nutrients in the sandy ground. She walked a bit further down the road before stopping in frustration to assess her options. Things were not making sense.

Laurina wondered if she had been deceived by Colonel Keren.

Why would the military send an operation here to this desolate place?

"Galicia!" Laurina yelled, cupping her mouth with her hands. "Major Flanagan!" Her voice echoed slightly in the empty air, and the only reply was a slight gust of wind that threw particles of sand in her face.

"Dammit Keren," she muttered in a low voice while brushing away the grit. "You sent me to a bloody ghost town."

Turning south, she continued down the road towards the water tower. She failed to notice the ominous shadow trailing behind her. The black form flew over the dry ground on soundless feet, like a panther approaching its prey.

Sensing no immediate danger, Laurina lazily strolled down the long road, gazing around at the scenery. Soon she realized she had stopped at the worn water tower. The cascading drops of clear water falling from its belly, made tiny splashing noises when they struck the surface of the puddle below it. Gingerly, she stepped into the puddle, walking toward its center. Cupping her hands, she gathered some of the liquid and splashed it on her face. Gathering more water, she rinsed her mouth and spit out the grit from the dust cloud in the warehouse. After tasting the cool liquid, she cupped her hands once more and hazarded a swallow. While it didn't slake her growing thirst, the coolness did provide her a bit of mild relief from the hot desert sun.

Gavrael ran lightly across the road like a wraith, stopping at the edge of a stand of scrub brush. His crystal blue eyes were as sharp as a hawk's, easily allowing him to observe the woman through the slit of his uniform's face mask. She had an oval face with delicate lips, and high cheekbones, and as she lifted her head and parted her lips to drink a handful of water, he could see that her slim figure belied a reservoir of underlying strength.

Under different circumstances, he would have considered her quite attractive.

As the SpecOps officer carefully advanced closer, he regarded the woman curiously as she brushed back a bit of her long auburn hair, revealing her slender neck. Her skin looked soft and smooth as if fashioned by a potter's hand, and the gesture itself was hauntingly familiar. One he had seen countless times in the past.

Quietly, he darted from his cover. As he moved, he caught sight of her eyes...

Emerald eyes that sparkled in the sunlight.

Suddenly he froze.

She was the spitting image of...

As Lieutenant Gavrael stopped his advance in wonder, he inadvertently kicked a small stone which flew through the air and struck against one of the rusted drums. Silently cursing his inattentiveness, he sprinted quickly toward his quarry.

Laurina heard something strike metal behind her. A sudden tingling sensation made its presence known within her body. Reacting instinctively, she ducked and rolled to the side, taking moderate cover behind one of the fifty-gallon drum lying nearby. As she rolled, she saw a black form fly past her, issuing a sidekick to the spot she had just vacated.

"I knew you would come sooner or later," the man in black said sadly, shaking his head. "How many terrorists will they send before they realize we will not let them destroy this place?"

Laurina stared perplexed at her would be attacker.

"Terrorist? I'm no bloody terrorist? What are you talking ab..."

The young Brit felt something cold grip her left arm. Before she could react, she felt both her arms tighten against her torso, while the cold sensation spread to both legs. In another moment, they too were drawn together, until she could do nothing but fall to the ground immobile.

"Just like clockwork," the man in black muttered.

As his SpecOp training dictated, his sidekick was actually a feint to distract his quarry, while he hurled a small metal ball at her, about the size of a marble. The SQD 30 was designed for close quarters use, to quickly subdue and immobilize an enemy. As it makes contact, six metal arms stronger than steel extend from its core, coiling tightly around the victim, to immediately restrict movement. While its use in the Aeternus military was still in the experimental stage, Gavrael was happy to see that the "Squid" performed as advertised.

"Get this thing off me!" Laurina screamed as she rolled back and forth on the withered grass and gravel.

The black-clad officer smiled grimly as he casually approached his squirming captive.

"All in good time. But first, I have a few questions. Who are you, and what is your mission?"

"Piss off, you bastard!" the redhead fired back. "Who the hell are you, and why are you doing this to me?" The tension of the metal arms around her body was becoming increasingly more uncomfortable until she began to feel it bruising her skin. The thought of being squeezed to death was more than the young Brit could bear.

"You're hurting me! Are you trying to kill me?"

"Calm yourself," the Aeternus soldier soothed. "I mean you no harm. If I wanted you dead, you would be so."

"So you attack me without provocation, and now all of a sudden you 'mean me no harm'? Yeah, rightie-o" she fired back sarcastically. Fully confined by the metal embrace of the strange device, the captive redhead stopped moving altogether, helpless and face down in the scrub grass.

"The Squid is designed to become tighter the more you struggle. If you cooperate with me, I will reduce the tension to a more bearable level."

Seeing that she had no choice in the matter, she sighed.

"You sure have a funny way of showing your peaceful intentions," she said grudgingly. "My name is Laurina."

"Good choice." Touching a small remote on his belt, he turned a tiny dial clockwise.

The thin metal arms supplied a bit of slack, and she relaxed visibly.

"Better?"

"Better," she replied.

"To answer your question, I am Lieutenant Gavrael of Aeternus. I am here in response to the terrorist activity that occurred within the warehouse."

"Well Gavrael, I'm not a terrorist I assure you," Laurina said. "I'm just a messenger from Keren."

"Is that so? So you deny any involvement with the terrorists Sinza Flanagan and Galicia Hawks?"

The color drained from the Brit's face at the mention of her sister's name.

Did he call Gal a terrorist? That can't be right. Gal hates violence. What the hell's going on around here?

"Please do us both a courtesy and refrain from any further denials Laurina. Your face betrays you. Besides, I heard you calling for them just moments ago. The fact is that these two people from your world have attempted to destroy the Interface, and with it, our contact with the Carbon world. Things will go a lot easier for both of us if you tell me the truth."
Laurina's jaw dropped at this unexpected revelation.

Two people from your world? Destroying the Interface? Our contact with the Carbon world? What the hell is he talking about? And why on earth would my sister and the Major do any of this? This must be the "difficulty" that Colonel Keren spoke about.

Laurina was in a fix. Without knowing the situation, there was no clear way she could respond without endangering her sister and Major Flanagan, as well as her mission to help them all get back home.

Plus if this bloke is calling them terrorists, and he's "responding to terrorist activity…" he's probably the enemy. And stupid me, I had to blurt out that I was a messenger from Keren! Loose lips sink ships, you twit!

"What exactly did they do?"
Gavrael's lips set a hard line. "That is classified information."
Laurina rolled her eyes.
"Of course it is," she muttered.

"Who did you say sent you?" he asked. "Karen who?"

She smiled sweetly. "That's classified information." Two can play this game. Frowning, the Aeternus officer grabbed her body firmly and rolled her onto her back.

"Not funny," he said. His abrupt manner startled Laurina. The time for fooling around was over.

"Look, I don't know what's going on here, but there's obviously been a misunderstanding," she offered. "I'm not interested in causing any trouble."

"Well, what I am interested in is the message that you are supposed to deliver to those two."

"Just information," she replied hastily.

After all, that is what the disk contains, right? She justified to herself.

So you are only a messenger?" Gavrael asked soberly. "Nothing more?"

"Well, of course, soldier boy!" Laurina replied with a hint of agitation. "I've got no technical expertise, I'm not in the military, and I don't even know what your stupid Interface is. I was sent here to New Mexico to deliver information and leave. Why the hell else would I be here?"

He looked at her soberly, puzzling a bit before answering.

"I'm not exactly sure where this New Mexico is, but I can assure you that this is not it."

"That's impossible," she said. "That's where they told me they were sending me."

"Then it seems that you missed the mark by a wide margin."

Panic began to swell within the heart of the trussed up redhead. It was difficult to believe with all of their technical sophistication, that Keren and the staff of his "special project" could make such an error. But it was possible.

Meanwhile, Lieutenant Gavrael was baffled by the woman's responses and explanations. She practically gave up information without a fight. A plant maybe? Judging by her manner and easy capture, that was highly unlikely. It was all but apparent that she was no operative. Not in the traditional sense anyway. Her level of naiveté regarding mission standards was astounding!

Something was very wrong here.

"You mean to tell me that you truly don't know where you are?" he asked her.

"Well mister know-it-all, if I'm not in New Mexico, then where the hell am I?"

The man regarded her soberly.

"You are...somewhere else."

Somewhere else? What does that mean?

"I am amazed that you Carbons are so disorganized."

"Carbons? W-what the hell is a Carbon?" Laurina stammered. "Look, you're not making any sense."

"Carbons. Short for Carbonites. That is the name given to people from your world."

"People from your wor--," Laurina started.

Gavrael read the puzzled expression on Laurina's face and sighed. This was going to be difficult.

"Let me see...how to best explain it...Well, the short answer is that you emerged through a gateway into another world."

The ground suddenly seemed to shift underneath Laurina's feet.

HAWKS EFFECT

Will continue with Episode 2

DIRE REVELATIONS

Read a preview:

Further inspection revealed an even bigger surprise, as Laurina caught sight of a young woman leisurely relaxing on a divan, sipping green liquid from a goblet. She was short in stature and wore a crimson silk jumpsuit with pleated sleeves and legs that billowed from her wrists and ankles. The frog buttons that would have normally come up to her chin, were only half fastened, revealing just enough of her slightly oversized breasts to attract attention. The woman straightened up when the door was opened and stretched her arms as if she had been sleeping. She glanced absently at the guards, then caught sight of the newcomer and smiled. It was not the condescending, benevolent smirk of Athena, but rather, a warm and genuine gesture of welcome.

"Wow! Company," the crimson-clad woman grinned as she stood from the divan. Honey colored hair poured around her shoulders as she straightened, and Laurina watched, mildly amused as she folded her outsized sleeves up on themselves while walking up to her. As she approached, the room's occupant smiled again, wrinkling her small freckled covered nose, as she grasped the redhead's hand like a lifeline. Satisfied that there would be no trouble between the two women, the black-robed guards turned smartly on their heels and exited the room while the heavy door closed behind them of its own accord.

"Boy, it's so nice to have a roommate after being alone for so long," the shorter woman gushed. Laurina for her part was a bit taken aback by her overt friendliness.

"Who are you and what am I doing here?" she asked perplexed.

Her new cellmate answered her in obvious glee.

"My name is Theodora Aellas, but everyone calls me Li'l Doro. Theodora sounds too pompous for me anyways."

This little sparkplug seems like the most open and down to earth person I've met since I've landed in this strange place. Perhaps she can give me some answers that make sense. Considering that Gavrael has his own military 'need to know' agenda, and that haughty bitch Athena barely acknowledges me at all, this just might be the break I've been looking for.

Coming November 2017

Rael Wissdorf was born in western Germany and lives near the city of Ulm. He studies Classical Guitar and Jazz Guitar as well as harmony and composition. He worked later as a Substitute Redactor in Chief for a Film magazine and raised up a video game company in Frankfurt/M. but went into writing soon after. Since 1999 he published two crime novels, several fantasy and science fiction books, as well as three collections of short stories.

Nicholas Hede was born in Wyoming, where he currently lives with his family. Since he was a boy he has been a voracious reader and prolific writer, having created dozens of admittedly horrible stories during his youth. He enjoys hunting and camping with his family and appreciates the privacy his home state affords.

Frank J Williams III was

born in Pittsburgh and was working for the University of Pittsburgh Medical Center while he attended classes in creative writing. His stories recalling neighborhood experiences were cited by an instructor as being reminiscent of August Wilsons works. When not writing, Frank enjoys his life as a Shamanic practitioner. A self-proclaimed Geek, and "granola making hippie," Frank and his wife Terry also own and manage their own organic foods business.